SPEAK OF THE DEVIL

14 Tales of Crimes and Their Punishments

SPEAK OF THE DEVIL

14 Tales of Crimes
and Their Punishments

Joe Gores

Five Star
Unity, Maine

Acknowledgments may be found on pp. 219–220.

Five Star Mystery
Published in conjunction with Tekno-Books & Ed Gorman.

September 1999

Standard Print Hardcover Edition.

First Edition

Five Star Standard Print Mystery Series.

The text of this edition is unabridged.

Set in 11 pt. Plantin by Minnie B. Raven.

Printed in the United States on permanent paper.

Library of Congress Cataloging-in-Publication Data

Gores, Joe, 1937–
 Speak of the devil : 14 tales of crimes and their punishments /
by Joe Gores.
  p. cm.
 ISBN 0-7862-2035-X (hc : alk. paper)
 1. Detective and mystery stories, American. 2. Punishment
Fiction. 3. Criminals Fiction. 4. Crime Fiction. I. Title.
PS3557.O75S64 1999
813′.54—dc21   99-27150

For Dori
with all my love

a few brief memories of
things past

TABLE OF CONTENTS

INTRODUCTION

I sold my first short story in 1957 to *Manhunt* for $65. At the time, I was living a few miles north of Papeete in Tahiti's Arue District, and that money paid the rent on my two-room thatch house for three months. I also sold my first magazine article, to *True Magazine* about living in Tahiti, that let me live there until I ran out of visa extensions at the end of the year.

My second short story sold the following year for $100, also to *Manhunt*. By then I was a buck private at the Pentagon, beginning a temporary career as a draftee writing biographies of Army generals.

For ten years after that first sale I wrote only short stories—with a batch of magazine articles tossed in that were nothing if not eclectic. One, for *The American Legion Magazine*, was titled "How to Protect Your Credit Rating."

My fiction was also eclectic. I did mainstream, science-fiction, fantasy, adventure, mystery, suspense, thrillers, and horror. I had 15 to 20 stories in the mail at all times, kept a log of stories submitted, and papered my bathroom with rejection slips. I also logged all stories sold and kept a year-by-year running total of money earned as a writer.

The totals were eclectic too: $490 in 1957; $100 in 1958; $170 in 1959; NO SALES in 1960. But 1961 was a banner year; eight stories to seven different magazines for a total of $1,115! I was learning how to do it.

For 12 of those early years I was a private investigator in San Francisco. First for L.A. Walker Company; then, from that banner year 1961 on, as a partner with Dave Kikkert in our own agency, David Kikkert & Associates. I quit full-time detective work in 1966 to try and make it as a writer, but Dave and I remained partners and friends until his death in 1983.

Writing reports for DKA's clients about my private eye and repo work taught me how to tell an exciting story containing the basic who, what, where, when, why, and how of all successful fiction (or newspaper reporting, for that matter). The files from these years at DKA have been the basis for a lifetime of stories and a series of novels. Mystery and suspense outsold anything else, so I naturally concentrated in that area.

But my first novel, *A Time of Predators*, was not a DKA File Novel about my fictionalized detective agency. After it sold to the great mystery editor Lee Wright at Random House in 1968, other novels followed and my short story production slowed. After I sold my first television script to *Kojak* in 1974, it slowed even further. I am not a fast writer; a short story can take me 3 to 6 weeks. If I was lucky, I could get $500 for it. By using the same 3 to 6 weeks to write an hour of episodic TV, at that time I could get $8,000.

I still write short stories, of course, because I dearly love reading and writing them. But the stories in *Speak of the Devil* span my most productive years in this field. Thus there is one story from the 1950s, four from the 1960s, five from the 1970s, three from the 1980s, and one from the 1990s.

All of the stories in this collection are mystery/suspense, but half of them could be said to have a mixed heritage. Three could be called fantasy, two could be considered horror, and two of them are rather hard-core science-fiction.

The short story is an unsurpassed training ground for

fiction writers, and in telling these tales I learned the principles of my craft. I mourn the demise of most of the markets beginning writers once could sell to.

My profession is to tell stories that people want to read, stories that grab you and scare you, enthrall you, make you laugh, trick you, make you unable to put them aside.

I hope these do.

Joe Gores
San Francisco
April 1, 1999

When I was in high school, a Catholic priest told me the climax of this story as the truth. He claimed to have seen the footprints. So many years later I came up with a pair of young, cynical, near-genius scientists to wrap around the basic tale. They set out to prove there is no good-dispensing God by proving there is no evil-dispensing Satan, with unforseen results.

SPEAK OF THE DEVIL

A year ago I would have challenged the inexorability of time. I would have proved, by adroit use of Einstein's clock paradox, that time is like all else relative. But since it has become an active physical entity like heavy water or the next martini—easy on the vermouth, please—I court its vaunted curative powers. Minutes, seconds, hours, creeping in their petty pace from day to day, have become like individual atoms and Angstroms and molecules to me. I try desperately to acknowledge that they knit up all the ravelled sleeves save death, yet know that their demise brings me inexorably closer to my own.

More than most men I fear that moment—not because oblivion might lie beyond it, but because oblivion might not. Or is this merely a morbid fancy born of long hours spent not talking with Pendennis?

Since the night of the storm he is incapable of speech; the doctors claim there is no physical reason, but to me the cause is the extreme *physicalness* of what happened. My own reaction has been much less flamboyant; each night I soak out consciousness of the passing hours—time again—and each afternoon I wait in the cool dim sanitarium for the ineffable word he never utters. Energy and matter? Natural law? Divine effulgence—yes, I would accept even that; but Pendennis says nothing. Hence the geometric progression of martinis.

I joined Pendennis' staff three months after my Ph.D.; my dissertation on particle energies (pion and lambda particles tracked as a single unit, Y^*, causing in an observed pion a recoil action $(K^- + \rho^+ \rightarrow Y^{*+-} + \pi^{-+})$ had got me the position of his assistant without even a personal interview. Conceptual nuclear physics is not a crowded field. Since I carried my individuality fiercely, like a falcon on my wrist, I arrived with the previous day's whiskers glinting golden on my narrow fox jaw, wearing windbreaker, striped T-shirt, Army fatigues—the old style with the baggy pockets outside—and strap sandals with a thong around my big toe.

The university was term-break deserted. In the Physical Sciences Building I wandered down bright corridors and stopped to peer out into golden California; since my graduate work had been under Hill at Illinois, a snowless land on a January morning could still hold my interest. I turned to the lone man clumping energetically by.

"Could you direct me to Dr. Pendennis' office?"

He was a large untidy person, wearing a baggy tweed suit the way a hippo wears its skin, and square-toed brogues more suited to a Celtic peat bog than vinyl and aluminum windows. With his bulbous nose, thick lips, and thinning curly hair he looked like an itinerant Irish poet.

"Dr. Pendennis' office," I repeated sharply. It woke him up.

"Who the hell are you, the new janitor?"

"Pendennis' new assistant. And they call them maintenance men."

"Bullshit," he said belligerently. I didn't know if he meant me or the janitors. He pulled a frowsty brier from his pocket and clamped it between strong incisors while his clear blue eyes crawled over me like staphylococci. "That would make you Shaw."

"Thomas Shaw."

"Doubting Thomas," he persisted.

"Because I never take a lesser man's word for anything." The gross-bodied boob was beginning to annoy me: just another glorified test-tube washer.

"Or a better man's word?"

"In my field I haven't met him."

He laughed out loud at that, putting his feet wide apart and crossing his arms on his chest like an I.R.A. man with a tommygun in the crook of his arm. For an instant something rare and almost shocking peeped from his pale blue eyes: naked intellect. His face was not any longer that of a faintly debauched cherub dancing on the head of a pin, but that of an Aquinas able to set the cherub whirling there.

"We'll get along. I'm Pendennis. Find me a way to convert the Regge poles quantum theory from math to physics and apply it to resonance particles, and the beer is on me."

Soon we were giving several nights a week to suds and argument. Pendennis opened lines of inquiry like a surgeon opening veins. Our lab experiments in the 72-inch liquid hydrogen bubble chamber gave us plenty to disagree about; I was using the university's high-speed digital computer to program the results. Facility with the IBM 709 had been one of the prerequisites for my position.

It was in the computer room one bright spring afternoon that I first realized Pendennis was an ultimates-seeker. To me life has always seemed a chemical accident, man an evolutionary sport, and phylum Annelida the end of it all; since I have maintained an implicit intellectual contempt for anyone who thinks otherwise, I was disconcerted to find a touch of that belief in Pendennis.

He came in and perched on a corner of the worktable so that his big fleshy buns cushioned under his weight and stretched taut the design of his perennial tweed. When I looked up he leaned over and said, straight-faced, "Tom, do you believe in God?"

I stared at him popeyed. "What the devil does that have to do with three-pion particle resonances?"

"Everything." He nodded his head several times like a courting grouse. "Scientific minds in the past have had to stop with the simplest element, hydrogen—molecular structure one proton, one electron—in trying to refute religionists who advocate a First Cause. But now we can destroy neutrons, break them down into protons and electrons through high-energy particle collisions, and build new atoms."

"We haven't done that in *this* shop," I pointed out. "Hell, we aren't here to prove or disprove a teleological cause for the universe, Pendennis. We two have a chance to do in physics what's never been done before. We can beat Alvarez or Fermi—but *not* if you're going to worry about ultimates."

A surprised look enlarged his face.

"Of course we'll beat them, Tom. But by going further than any physicist before us, we're going to show there's no pink frosting on the cake of creation. Our work will demonstrate that from a collision—an inevitable collision—of opposing forces of energy came the first cosmic matter. Then, once most of the earth's free hydrogen escaped from the atmosphere, methane, ammonia, and water eventually began producing the adenine necessary for life. After that came the eons of evolutionary experiment and systematization which religionists call Natural Law."

The man amazed me: an ultimates-seeker. His search for a scientifically explainable universe equated with the Christian existentialist's search for God, or the latent hysteric's hope that psychiatry is the key to his emotional instability. With his debauched poet's face and Wolfean physique, Pendennis shuffled in his toed-out sloth's shuffle after his ideal universe: a clean well-lighted place with only sphere music (pure energy) flowing through in directly measureable waves like light corpuscles through an oscilloscope.

With my fair skin, flaxen hair, and narrow fox face, wearing my T-shirt and fatigues with a crazy elegance, I tried with delicate hands like Eliot's scuttling claws to fend off *my* universe: a disordered place of chance beginnings where only the ingrained habits of evolution prevented women from giving birth to calves' heads; a universe with no meaning outside the individual lives, in micro-seconds, of its subatomic particles.

During the summer months we charted for the first time in history the energy distribution of a negative K meson and a proton by adapting the Halitz graph to show two relatively strong peaks in the plot of the negative pion and a single stronger peak in that of the positive pion. Since this distribution is consistent with the reaction producing two rather than three particles $(K^- + \rho^+ \rightarrow Y^* + \pi)$, and the strongest peak showed an average lifetime for Y^* of 10^{-23} (a hundred-thousandth of a billion-billionth second), the publication of our conclusions created quite a stir.

All this, of course, was before the storm and even before Pendennis' natal day, when I gave him the Ouija board as a joke.

The week after *Scientific American* carried a summation of our findings, Pendennis invited me over for a birthday bottle of Rémy Martin VSOP cognac. Turning toward his place through the undergraduates lacing the narrow street, I spotted a little hobby shop still open. It was one of those places that smell of model airplane dope and varnish; I was just deciding on a model kit of H.M.S. *Beagle*, the brigantine on which Darwin collected data for *Origin of Species* in 1831, when I spotted the Ouija board and bought that instead.

"Sorry I couldn't get it wrapped properly."

"What is it?" His homely face was wreathed in smiles as he ripped off the brown paper wrapping. He was as excited as a kid at Christmas.

"Ouija board. The name comes from the French 'yes' and the German 'yes' combined—oui—ja. If you're attuned to the great beyond it spells things out for you."

He was touchingly delighted. "Does it work?"

"Not for a cynical scientist like me, but some people who ought to know better swear this thingamajig here—the counter—moves of its own volition across the board and spells out answers to questions."

"I'll be damned. What sort of things do you ask it?"

"Hell, I don't know. Is there a God?"

As kids we had always asked how old our mothers were or what our girl friends' names were, but Pendennis took me seriously. "Great! We can try to have a chat with the Old Gentleman!"

All we got was an aimless circling by the counter, but by midnight each abortive attempt left us squeaking like mice—*in vino hilaritas*. So I suggested to Pendennis, "Ask for results on this tau-meson decay study we're starting."

He did, fingers lightly grasping the counter; a big blindfolded untidy man with his belly over his pants and sweat soaking through his shirt. I often wondered if he didn't seek neatness in his physical universe because he had none in his physical self—only gross flesh wrapped around an amazing brain. As I was putting *Night on Bald Mountain* on the hi-fi he yelled from across the room.

"Tom, the damn thing just shot across the board in a straight line!"

I looked: the counter rested firmly on *I*. As I was telling him about it, the counter sidled over to *N*. *IN*. In what?

"Indium: In," I suggested. "Atomic number forty-nine. Atomic weight 114.76. Density 7.28."

Pendennis was giggling under his blindfold. "Inconsistent systems of linear algebraic equations."

"Infundubulum."

"Wait a minute!" he cried, "There it goes again!"

"Head it off at the pass!" But it had already stopped on *S*.

"INS. Insecta? That's it. A class of the phylum Arthropoda, the largest taxonomic division of the animal kingdom, 450,000 species."

"Actually it's spelling instant coffee," I said. "A hint that—"

"International News Service. Due to my fame as a conceptual physicist, *INS* will make Pendennis a household— hey, it's moving again!"

A. Then *N*. Then a six-minute wait so that we almost decided it had stalled on *INSAN;* but then in rapid succession came *I, T,* and *Y.*

"Here it is, hot off the presses," I said. *"INSANITY."*

"In a way it makes sense, Tom." He was removing his blindfold. "Very straightforward: if we continue our work we'll go buggo."

"Maybe you already have. You can't seriously believe—"

"It spelled out a word," he said, cognac-stubborn.

"*You* spelled out the word. Your subconscious, working from memory of the letter placement on the board, moved your hands and the counter under them to various letters."

"You accept that as the explanation of a Ouija board?"

"I do."

"Not me. Not yet." He leaned back, crossed his legs, jammed his foul dead pipe between his teeth, and stared at the board. "I wonder . . ."

Once, from an interest in the history of mathematics, I was led into Blaise Pascal's *Pensées*. I've forgotten all I can, but one thing stuck: he said that when you start looking for God you have already found Him. Pendennis was looking for a rational explanation of the universe that would dispense with God—which meant he really thought he would find one. The trouble with that is that an intelligent and honest man invariably ends up at the inexplicable. Has to. Always will.

He began showing up with studies in clinical psychology—the subconscious mind, of course—and soon was keeping Freud's *Interpretations of Dreams* on his desk. Jung's *Memories, Dreams, Reflections* was often propped up against the toaster for ingestion with his morning eggs, and the bookshelves in the living room, sprawling and untidy as Pendennis himself, began bristling with Adler, Brill, Bergson, and Krafft-Ebing. On the bottom shelf was something called simply *Dianetics*.

Even in California you get a feeling of fall in the air. A few leaves change, the evenings get crisper, and on the quiet streets of a university town, fresh-fallen walnuts crunch underfoot or plunk off the tops of parked cars. There was a change in Pendennis, too.

"Congratulations, Pendennis! For a whole week you haven't mentioned the id, your psychoses, or my sex drive as the reason I had two pieces of chocolate cake at lunch."

"It's that damned Ouija board, Tom—I had to find out if the subconscious mind works it. After studying the data I accept that, but—" He nodded and snapped his fingers. "There are so damned many people who *wouldn't* accept it, who still would claim it was some supernatural agency."

"Nothing you can do about that. It's irrational, a perversion of common sense by religious sense."

He grunted. "I've got nothing against religion, but it's so blasted self-perpetuating. If science could once clear away all the nonsense about good and evil, God and the devil, man could transform his own destiny—merely by relying on himself alone."

"Nothing much you can do about it," I repeated.

He stared at me piercingly, then suddenly grinned all over his fat face and heaved himself from his easy chair. "I've been waiting to spring this on you. C'mon in the bedroom—I think you'll be interested."

In the bedroom there was a strong smell of astringent soap coupled with a faint odor of incense. All the furniture had been removed and two concentric circles—the outer one with a diameter of about nine feet and the inner one with about seven—had been painted on the bare hardwood floor. In the space between were some strange letters.

"Hebrew alphabet," he explained airily.

"Pendennis, have you gone absolutely fruitcake? What the—"

"And the square inside the inner circle—see? Very important. The upper point has to face directly east so the cross inside will point the right way. And the Star of David that I've superimposed—"

19

"I need a drink," I cut in hollowly. With a glass in one hand I waggled my free fingers at him. "Okay, give. What the hell is it?"

"A Sacred Pentacle." He said it with a straight face.

"To call up the devil?"

He ignored the sarcasm in my voice. "No, this one's to cast spells and curses."

"And you're saying that Satan will come and—"

He shook his head vehemently. "If you're after Satan himself, draw a circle around your triangle and hold a hazel wand cut with a new knife at sunrise from a tree which has never borne fruit."

"Well, I'll be damned. Pendennis, there are only two possibilities—either this is some elaborate leg pull or you actually have wigged out. If it isn't a joke—"

"It's no joke."

"Then you're serious. Then—"

"But when I say I've been doing this seriously for the past two weeks I'm not saying I expect—or ever did expect—anything to come of it." He leaned forward to pour himself another cognac, leaned back, waved an arm, and said, "Ultimates."

"You dignify that cheap hocus-pocus in there as an ultimate?"

He stoked up his pipe and gestured through the smoke. "Tom, it all ties in: energy as the origin of the universe, the subconscious mind in relation to the Ouija board, that pentacle in the next room. We're both agreed that man would be a hell of a lot better off if he had never invented God in the first place, right?"

"Right."

"Okay. Then give me a scientifically acceptable proof that there is no God." When I just sat there looking at him, he waved his pipe triumphantly. "See? They *start out* with something not susceptible to proof. They don't even have to be logical." He tapped me on the knee with his pipestem. "Now: give me your impressions of the devil."

"You mean Satan?"

"Any name you want: Lucifer, Beelzebub, Astoreth."

I thought for a while. "First, he doesn't exist. Second, if he did, he would be an Edwardian gentleman with a gold-tipped cane and a bit of goatee, lighting thin cheroots without the aid of matches."

"That's interesting." He nodded several times. "My own idea is that Satan was the first scientist. Look at the sin for which he was banished—an intellectual one. He tempts Adam and Eve not with licentiousness but with knowledge. Churches call him Prince of Earth—the physical universe. I take him as a proto-Faust, an inquirer. Now, how does Christianity take him?"

"As a force of evil. The powers of darkness—"

"As an *individual*." He grinned, squirrel-cheeked. "In the past the pentacle has been accepted as *the* way to summon Satan—see *The Key of Solomon*, *The Book of Enoch*, or *The Great Grimoire of Honorius III*. In *The New Testament* we have herds of possessed swine running over a cliff, and Satan appearing *in person* to tempt Christ in Matthew Four and transform himself into an angel of light in Two Corinthians. Consider the Inquisition: expression of a deadly serious belief in demonic possession of the person."

"Wait a minute!" I burst out. "I see where you're heading, but Christianity can claim they've been speaking of the devil *symbolically*—the old Scholastic line that evil is merely a good gone wrong."

He shook his head vigorously, so that his belly and the bulbs of his loose pectorals bounced under his white shirt.

"They can't. Augustine and Aquinas both posit his existence as an individual, *not* as a disembodied force; and today the Catholic mass ends with the words '. . . by the divine power thrust into hell Satan and the other evil spirits who wander through the world seeking the ruin of souls.' No, Tom, they can't back out."

"But *two weeks* of mumbling incantations, Pendennis!"

He heaved himself from the sagging easy chair whose springs had long since surrendered to his weight, and brought back from the bookcase a flat manila folder. He parked his broad buns once more.

"The only way to prove they didn't work. But that isn't enough. Take a look at these—can you program them for the 709 computer?"

Inside the folder, on several sheets of onion skin in Pendennis' neat copperplate, were a complex series of mathematical symbols. When I finally nodded he began to beam.

"What you have there is a virtually complete abstract of every known spell and incantation to summon Satan, all reduced to mathematical formulas. Now all we have to do is program the symbols for the digital computer, thereby reducing the factor of human error to zero, and if my symbols are correct and your program logical, Satan *must* appear."

"And if no goateed gent after an eternal lease on our souls shows up, you believe that will prove he doesn't exist."

"That's what I believe. Scientifically demonstrating that there is no personal entity devoting itself to evil may not disprove the existence of its counterfoil, a personal God devoted to good—but it sure will raise questions."

That's when I started to laugh. Staring into Pendennis' sweat-stippled face and listening to his solemn tones, considering he was one of the world's most brilliant physicists, made not laughing impossible. I stuck out my hand, still choking. "I'm your boy, Pendennis."

We decided that to the Edwardian-gentleman proto-Faust we had conceived, the computer room itself would be acceptable. No belladonna, no heavy drapes, no musk or black masses necessary. I wanted to finish the program by Halloween, however.

"A ritualistic bow to the past," I explained to Pendennis. "This ought to be what a midnight walk through a grave-yard is to a kid."

"How do you mean?"

"We know nothing will happen but we should still manage to scare the hell out of ourselves at least once on the way through. Oh, can you line up an oscilloscope for to-morrow night?"

"Sure, but what are you going to use it for?"

I took him over to the 709's central computing unit, a squat gray metal box, waist-high with all the switches and rows of lights usually lampooned in cartoons and featured in science-fiction films.

"A program, Pendennis, is merely a logical arrangement of instructions to the machine. You already had the incantations reduced to symbols; I transferred them to a set of key-punch cards, then cut instructions on another set of cards and assembled them into a self-loading program. Tomorrow night I will run your symbolic representations of the incantations through central computing to core storage, that big metal box over there—a sort of super filing system with storage 'locations' from 00001 to 77777."

"Like a filing cabinet with seventy-seven thousand seven hundred and seventy-seven drawers?"

"Close enough. Once I've loaded—stored—each incantation at a separate location in core storage, I will then load

23

the program itself—the logical set of instructions to the machine—into this third box off to the left that's known as the card reader. The program will order the computer to follow instructions sequentially."

He waved an impatient fleshy hand. "But the oscilloscope—"

"Patience, Pendennis. Once the incantations are at the proper locations in core storage and the instructions—the program—are in the card reader, I push the *logical start button.* This tells the computer: *go to 'begin' of instructions and START PROCESSING.* Instruction A of the program tells central computing to get the first incantation from its location in core storage. When it does, I want the 'shape' of that incantation flashed through the oscilloscope. We can sit here in the dark—more spooky that way—and watch the pattern of light corpuscles on the screen just as if we were watching a test pattern on a television screen."

"Why is that necessary?"

"How can a man with a supposedly brilliant mind be so obtuse? Getting the incantation from its location and putting it into the operating register corresponds to chanting and waving your wand in your pentacle. By flashing it on the oscilloscope screen—"

He was nodding. "Sure. We have to have an actual release of energy to give Satan something physical through which to materialize."

"Right. Once the incantation at the first location has been used, the machine automatically goes on to instruction B."

"Which is?"

"To go to 00666 in core storage, designated as *LOCATION DEVIL.*"

"666—the Mark of the Beast in *Revelations.* Satan will be there?"

"If the incantation has worked. If there is no change at 00666, the machine passes to instruction C, which orders it to 00333, *LOCATION NO-DEVIL*—a standing instruction for the on-line printer, this fourth box over here, to print *YOUR NUMBER DOES NOT ANSWER*. After that the machine goes to instruction D, an order to begin the whole process again for the second incantation. After we've used them all, the computer goes to the terminal location and receives an order for the on-line printer: *I DO NOT EXIST.* Then the machine shuts itself off."

"What if there should actually be some change at *LOCATION DEVIL?*"

"Then the on-line printer will give us *HERE I AM*. One other thing. Because new programs often have 'bugs' in them—minor illogicities which in this case might conceivably make the computer print *HERE I AM* even though Satan isn't at *LOCATION DEVIL*—I've built the program so that the machine will go to *LOCATION MATERIALIZE* any time it prints *HERE I AM*. This orders it back to *LOCATION DEVIL* once more to flash the pattern of anything which might be there to the oscilloscope. Then, assuming nothing is there, it goes back into sequence."

When I was halfway down the walk the first spears of rain began lancing down, so I went back for my poncho. By the time I had crossed the campus to the Physical Sciences Building it was a real Halloween night—howling wind and rain lashing my legs. And as I used my key on the side entrance, lightning flashed vividly down the inky night and thunder pulsed and roared in a far corner of the sky.

Light spilled across the third-floor corridor from the computer-room door; inside Pendennis was perched shapelessly over his favorite corner of the worktable, all tweeds and tobacco and wet-wool smell.

"The small craft warnings will be up on the coast," he said over the rim of his cognac glass. "Gale force winds, by the radio."

"I didn't see any hobgoblin outfits on the way over."

"And won't. Too wet. Too late, too—after eleven." He stopped as lightning seared the windows; the crunch of thunder punctuated his braying donkey laugh. "Too late for real hobgoblins, too, Tom. Mankind's impressionable youth has mellowed into cynical middle age. I drink to the passing of the Age of Belief."

While warming up the machine and storing the incantations I downed a stiff cognac. "At least the weather is cooperating even if Satan won't. Pendennis, it's a night for hell to breathe contagions."

He grinned. "Thomas—" He raised his glass as lightning flickered the windows, and thunder boomed. "—to failure."

"To failure."

At one minute to midnight the program cards were in the reader and Pendennis walked over to the light switch. I put my finger on the start button of the 709. Only the shush of rain marred the silence.

"Thirty seconds," said Pendennis.

Half a dozen televised Canaveral launchings flashed through my mind. "No countdowns, please," I said.

"Fifteen seconds. When the lights go out, you're on."

"Speak of the devil," I said.

Darkness. Start button. Cards flipping through the reader. In the rain-spattered silence the oscilloscope screen glowed greenly. Light green patterns, the first incantation, wriggled across it as Pendennis groped his way back to his seat. By the glow I picked out the words of the on-line printer's first clacked message.

"YOUR NUMBER DOES NOT ANSWER," I read.

"It made a damned pretty pattern. Scratch Number One."

"And Number Two." The printer was repeating the message.

I knew then—had known all along but had subconsciously ignored it—that nothing was going to happen. In a way I felt cheated. I said, "Same for Number Three. Some set of incantations *you* picked, Pendennis."

"Best on the market, my boy," he said cheerfully.

After all, he was being proved right.

"Same for—hey, what the—?"

The printer had blurted *HERE I AM*.

I grunted gloomily as the printer belched *MATERIALIZE*.

"I must have programmed a bug into it. I'll turn on the lights and—"

"This pattern's gone crazy!" exclaimed Pendennis.

"That'll teach us," I said, fumbling my way to the door. "I'll probably have to spend two days getting the machine cleared."

But as my fingers touched the light switch the darkness was split by a sudden tremendous sheet of fire, a searing flash across my eyes. The entire building seemed to rise, turn, buckle, the floor seemed to heave like the surface of the sea when tsunami shock waves pass through it. Thunder roared—gigantic, shocking, unutterable.

Then dead silence. Blackness.

Pendennis said in a desperately normal voice, "This building must have been struck by lightning."

I felt a strange tingling relief. "For a second I thought—"

"This building—" he began again; then glass shattered, and there was a tremendous roaring, a sensation of horrible goat-stench, a scorching corposant white-hot-black whiz-zing, a furnace-blast stink in my face—and a hairy shoulder sent me sprawling. *Hairy?*

"—been struck—"

In whirling blackness his futile litany of rationality was more grotesque than the inner-glowing shape, fireball, thing, already gone; the fluorescents began to glow weakly.

"—lightning—" His terminal word hung lifeless.

Scrambling to my feet I found the floor unbuckled and no windows smashed: but the oscilloscope screen was sharded to dust across the floor.

Pendennis was standing in front of the gray, settled mound of metal where the 709 had—

The 709.

—melted.

Running glowing goatlike . . . Pendennis had been directly in front of the oscilloscope. He had seen it.

"Pendennis—"

Pendennis was maintaining silence. Doubting Thomas— I worked hard at it. A freak lightning had shorted the electricity, melting the computer. Pendennis, a salt image, was now trembling.

He had seen it.

Damn it, no! Lightning! Reek of a billion matches. No! Lightning. It must have been!

I pounded my clenched fist on the worktable until the knuckle of the little finger was mashed flat and bloody. Edwardian gentleman? Proto-Faust? The Shaggy One—Greek goat-god Dionysos, Egyptian death-god Set. Goat-stink, brimstone-stink . . .

Lightning?

Then why the clots of tumbled steaming dung on the floor?

I must sweep it out—like manure from Augean's stable. I must. Impossible to explain. I must forget. But what if I *had* seen the face—as Pendennis had . . .

No! I must not accept. Must clean up. Must . . .

Tracks.

I saw the tracks, shoulder-level, all the way around the room, still faintly smoking. I reached out. On the walls? *In* the walls? Black three-toed clawmarks burned into the restfully green plaster. Ten feet between tracks.

No! Must not accept. Freak of Natural Law.

I led Pendennis like a trained Himalaya bear down to the chem lab on the second floor and perched him on a stool, baby-obedient—doughy flesh, with no yeast of spirit to work within. Fire with fire. Must get thermite. White-hot burning, stark intensity of flashbulb, all-consuming, all-melting, like lightning, like Satan, like metal, like a 709 computer. Scorching out three-toes antediluvian tracks. If no one else saw, would I have to accept ?

No. Must not accept. *Time.* I saw my life avidly lapping up seconds, minutes, hours, days, weeks, years, *lifetime*—one lifetime to be traversed, tightrope over the abyss, burdened with that knowledge—no, I must not accept—to . . . to what? White hairs to a quiet grave? Or misshapen cloven-footed thing?

Leaving Pendennis in the chem lab, I started back upstairs with the thermite, precious as philosopher's stone, bent on necessary fire. I knew inexorable time and I feared it, more than most men; it was rushing me toward that final wall beyond which might lie—Eternity.

And knowing that, I wondered if perhaps Pendennis, in his quiet insane retreat to that inner vacuum where no voice sounds and no time flows—if Pendennis were not the luckier of us after all.

I wrote this story shortly after Caryl Chessman's execution had stirred anti-death penalty sentiment, and a friend had told me of witnessing an execution because he thought it would be "a gas"—literally. He had been badly shaken by the experience, but was too much of a swinger to let it show. So I recounted the tale of this horrific event in his cool, hip argot.

THE SECOND COMING

"But fix thy eyes upon the valley: for the river of blood draws nigh, in which boils every one who by violence injures other."

Canto XII, 46–48

THE INFERNO OF DANTE ALIGHIERI

I've thought about it a lot, man; like why Victor and I made that terrible scene out there at San Quentin, putting ourselves on that it was just for kicks. Victor was hung up on kicks; they were a thing with him. He was a sharp dark-haired cat with bright eyes, built lean and hard like a French skin-diver. His old man dug only money, so he'd always had plenty of bread. We got this idea out at his pad on Potrero Hill—a penthouse, of course—one afternoon when we were lying around on the sun-porch in swim trunks and drinking gin.

"You know, man," he said, "I have made about every scene in the world. I have balled all the chicks, red and yellow and black and white, and I have gotten high on muggles, bluejays, redbirds, and mescaline. I have even tried the white stuff a time or two. But—"

"You're a goddamned tiger, dad."

"—but there is one kick I've never had, man."

When he didn't go on I rolled my head off the quart gin bottle I was using for a pillow and looked at him. He was giving me a shot with those hot, wild eyes of his.

"So like what is it?"

"I've never watched an execution."

I thought about it a minute, drowsily. The sun was so hot it was like nailing me right to the air mattress. Watching an execution. Seeing a man go through the wall. A groovy idea for an artist.

"Too much," I murmured. "I'm with you, dad."

The next day, of course, I was back at work on some abstracts for my first one-man show and had forgotten all about it; but that night Victor called me up.

"Did you write to the warden up at San Quentin today, man? He has to contact the San Francisco police chief and make sure you don't have a record and aren't a psycho and are useful to the community."

So I went ahead and wrote the letter because even sober it still seemed a cool idea for some kicks; I knew they always need twelve witnesses to make sure that the accused isn't sneaked out the back door or something at the last minute like an old Jimmy Cagney movie. Even so, I lay dead for two months before the letter came. The star of our show would be a stud who'd broken into a house trailer near Fort Ord to rape this Army lieutenant's wife, only right in the middle of it she'd started screaming so he'd put a pillow over her face to keep her quiet until he could finish. But she'd quit breathing. There were eight chicks on the jury and I think like three of them got broken ankles in the rush to send him to the gas chamber. Not that I cared. Kicks, man.

Victor picked me up at seven-thirty in the morning, an hour before we were supposed to report to San Quentin. He was wearing this really hip Italian import, and fifty-dollar shoes, and a narrow-brim hat with a little feather in it, so all he needed was a briefcase to be Chairman of the Board. The top was down on the Mercedes, cold as it was, and when he saw my black suit and hand-knit tie he flashed this crazy white-toothed grin you'd never see in any Director's meeting.

"*Too much,* killer! If you'd like comb your hair you could pass for an undertaker coming after the body."

Since I am a very long, thin cat with black hair always hanging in my eyes, who fully dressed weighs as much as a medium-sized collie, I guess he wasn't too far off. I put a pint of José Cuervo in the side pocket of the car and we split. We were both really turned on: I mean this senseless, breathless hilarity as if we'd just heard the world's funniest joke. Or were just going to.

It was one of those chilly California brights with blue sky and cold sunshine and here and there a cloud like Mr. Big was popping Himself a cap down beyond the horizon. I dug it all: the sail of a lone early yacht out in the Bay like a tossed-away paper cup; the whitecaps flipping around out by Angel Island like they were stoned out of their minds; the top down on the 300-SL so we could smell salt and feel the icy bite of the wind. But beyond the tunnel on U.S. 101, coming down towards Marin City, I felt a sudden sharp chill as if a cloud had passed between me and the sun, but none had; and then I dug for the first time what I was actually doing.

Victor felt it, too, for he turned to me and said, "Must maintain cool, dad."

"I'm with it."

San Quentin Prison, out on the end of its peninsula, looked like a sprawled ugly dragon sunning itself on a rock;

we pulled up near the East Gate and there were not even any birds singing. Just a bunch of quiet cats in black, Quakers or Mennonites or something, protesting capital punishment by their silent presence as they'd done ever since Chessman had gotten his out there. I felt dark frightened things move around inside me when I saw them.

"Let's fall out right here, dad," I said in a momentary sort of panic, "and catch the matinee next week."

But Victor was in kicksville, like desperate to put on all those squares in the black suits. When they looked over at us he jumped up on the back of the bucket seat and spread his arms wide like the Sermon on the Mount. With his tortoise-shell shades and his flashing teeth and that suit which had cost three yards, he looked like Christ on his way to Hollywood.

"Whatsoever ye do unto the least of these, my brethren, ye do unto me," he cried in this ringing apocalyptic voice.

I grabbed his arm and dragged him back down off the seat "For Christ sake, man, cool it!"

But he went into high laughter and punched my arm with feverish exuberance, and then jerked a tiny American flag from his inside jacket pocket and began waving it around above the windshield. I could see the sweat on his forehead.

"It's worth it to live in this country!" he yelled at them.

He put the car in gear and we went on. I looked back and saw one of those cats crossing himself. It put things back in perspective: they were from nowhere. The Middle Ages. Not that I judged them: that was their scene, man. Unto every cat what he digs the most.

The guard on the gate directed us to a small wooden building set against the outside wall, where we found five other witnesses. Three of them were reporters, one was a fat cat smoking a .45 caliber stogy like a politician from Sacramento, and the last was an Army type in lieutenant's bars, his belt buckle and insignia looking as if he'd been up all night with a can of Brasso.

A guard came in and told us to surrender everything in our pockets and get a receipt for it. We had to remove our shoes, too; they were too heavy for the fluoroscope. Then they put us through this groovy little room one-by-one to x-ray us for cameras and so on; they don't want anyone making the Kodak scene while they're busy dropping the pellets. We ended up inside the prison with our shoes back on and with our noses full of that old prison detergent-disinfectant stink.

The politician type, who had those cold slitted eyes like a Sherman tank, started coming on with rank jokes: but everyone put him down, hard, even the reporters. I guess nobody but fuzz ever gets used to executions. The Army stud was at parade rest with a face so pale his freckles looked like a charge of shot. He had reddish hair.

After a while five guards came in to make up the twelve required witnesses. They looked rank, as fuzz always do, and got off in a corner in a little huddle, laughing and gassing together like a bunch of kids kicking a dog. Victor and I sidled over to hear what they were saying.

"Who's sniffing the eggs this morning?" asked one.

"I don't know, I haven't been reading the papers." He yawned when he answered.

"Don't you remember?" urged another, "it's the guy who smothered the woman in the house trailer. Down in the Valley by Salinas."

"Yeah. Soldier's wife; and he was raping her and . . ."

Like dogs hearing the plate rattle, they turned in unison toward the Army lieutenant; but just then more fuzz came in to march us to the observation room. We went in a column of twos with a guard beside each one, everyone unconsciously in step as if following a cadence call. I caught myself listening for measured mournful drum rolls.

The observation room was built right around the gas chamber, with rising tiers of benches for extras in case business was brisk. The chamber itself was hexagonal; the three walls in our room were of plate glass with a waist-high brass rail around the outside like the rail in an old-time saloon. The three other walls were steel plate, with a heavy door, rivet-studded, in the center one, and a small observation window in each of the others.

Inside the chamber were just these two massive chairs, probably oak, facing the rear walls side-by-side; their backs were high enough to come to the nape of the neck of anyone sitting in them. Under each was like a bucket that I knew contained hydrochloric acid. At a signal the executioner would drop sodium cyanide pellets into a chute; the pellets would roll down into the bucket; hydrocyanic acid gas would form; and the cat in the chair would be wasted.

The politician type, who had this rich fruity baritone like Burl Ives, asked why they had two chairs.

"That's in case there's a double-header, dad," I said.

"You're kidding." But by his voice the idea pleased him. Then he wheezed plaintively: "I don't see why they turn the chairs away—we can't even watch his face while it's happening to him."

He was a true rank genuine creep, right out from under a rock with the slime barely dry on his scales; but I wouldn't have wanted his dreams. I think he was one of those guys who tastes the big draught many times before he swallows it.

We milled around like cattle around the chute when they

smell the blood from inside and know they're somehow involved; then we heard sounds and saw the door in the back of the chamber swing open. A uniformed guard appeared to stand at attention, followed by a priest dressed all in black like Zorro, with his face hanging down to his belly button. He must have been a new man, because he had trouble maintaining his cool: just standing there beside the guard he dropped his little black book on the floor like three times in a row.

The Army cat said to me, as if he'd wig out unless he broke the silence: "They . . . have it arranged like a stage play, don't they?"

"But no encores," said Victor hollowly.

Another guard showed up in the doorway and they walked in the condemned man. He was like sort of a shock. You expect a stud to *act* like a murderer: I mean, cringe at the sight of the chair because he knows this is it, there's finally no place to go, no appeal to make, or else bound in there full of cheap bravado and go-to-hell. But he just seemed mildly interested, nothing more.

He wore a white suit with the sleeves rolled up, suntan that looked Army issue, and no tie. Under thirty, brown crewcut hair—the terrible thing is that I cannot even remember the features on his face, man. The closest I could come to a description would be that he resembled the Army cat right there beside me with his nose to the glass.

The one thing I'll never forget is that stud's hands. He'd been on Death Row all these months, and here his hands were still red and chapped and knobby, as if he'd still been out picking turnips in the San Joaquin Valley. Then I realized: I was thinking of him in the past tense.

Two fuzz began strapping him down in the chair. A broad leather strap across the chest, narrower belts on the arms and legs. God they were careful about strapping him in. I mean they wanted to make sure he was comfortable. And all the time he was talking with them. Not that we could hear it, but I suppose it went *that's fine, fellows, no, that strap isn't too tight, gee, I hope I'm not making you late for lunch.*

That's what bugged me, he was so damned apologetic! While they were fastening him down over that little bucket of oblivion, that poor dead lonely son of a bitch twisted around to look over his shoulder at us, and he *smiled.* I mean if he'd had an arm free he might have *waved!* One of the fuzz, who had white hair and these sad gentle eyes like he was wearing a hair shirt, patted him on the head on the way out. No personal animosity, son, just doing my job.

After that the tempo increased, like your heartbeat when you're on a black street at three a.m. and the echo of your own footsteps begins to sound like someone following you. The warden was at one observation window, the priest and the doctor at the other. The blackrobe made the sign of the cross, having a last go at the condemned, but he was digging only Ben Casey. Here was this M.D. cat who'd taken the Hippocratic Oath to preserve life, waving his arms around like a TV director to show that stud the easiest way to *die.*

Hold your breath, then breathe deeply: you won't feel a thing. Of course hydrocyanic acid gas melts your guts into a red-hot soup and burns out every fiber in the lining of your lungs, but you won't be really feeling it as you jerk around: that'll just be raw nerve endings.

Like they should have called *his* the Hypocritical Oath.

So there we were, three yards and half an inch of plate glass apart, with us staring at him and him by just turning his head able to stare right back: but there were a million light years between the two sides of the glass. He didn't turn. He was shrived and strapped in and briefed on how to die, and he was ready for the fumes. I found out afterwards that he had even willed his body to medical research.

I did a quick take around.

Victor was sweating profusely, his eyes glued to the window.

The politician was pop-eyed, nose pressed flat and belly indented by the brass rail, pudgy fingers like plump garlic sausages smearing the glass on either side of his head. A look on his face, already, like that of a stud making it with a chick.

The reporters seemed ashamed, as if someone had caught them peeking over the transom into the ladies' john.

The Army cat just looked sick.

Only the fuzz were unchanged, expending no more emotion on this than on their targets after rapid-fire exercises at the range.

On no face was there hatred.

Suddenly, for the first time in my life, I was part of it. I wanted to yell out *STOP!* We were about to gas this stud and *none of us wanted him to die!* We've created this society and we're all responsible for what it does, but none of us as individuals is willing to take that responsibility. We're like that Nazi cat at Nuremberg who said that everything would have been all right if they'd only given him more ovens.

The warden signaled. I heard gas whoosh up around the chair.

The condemned man didn't move. He was following doctor's orders. Then he took the huge gulping breath the M.D. had pantomimed. All of a sudden he threw this tremendous convulsion, his body straining up against the straps, his head slewed around so I could see his eyes were shut tight and his lips were pulled back from his teeth. Then he started panting like a baby in an oxygen tent, swiftly and shallowly. Only it wasn't oxygen his lungs were trying to work on.

The lieutenant stepped back smartly from the window, blinked, and puked on the glass. His vomit hung there for an instant like a phosphorus bomb burst in a bunker; then two fuzz were supporting him from the room and we were all jerking back from the mess. All except the politician. He hadn't even noticed: he was in Henry Millersville, getting his sex kicks the easy way.

I guess the stud in there had never dug that he was supposed to be gone in two seconds without pain, because his body was still arched up in that terrible bow, and his hands were still claws. I could see the muscles standing out along the sides of his jaws like marbles. Finally he flopped back and just hung there in his straps like a machine-gunned paratrooper.

But that wasn't the end. He took another huge gasp, so I could see his ribs pressing out against his white shirt. After that one, twenty seconds. We decided that he had cut out.

Then another gasp. Then nothing. Half a minute nothing.

Another of those final terrible shuddering racking gasps. At last: all through. All used up. Making it with the angels.

But then he did it *again*. Every fiber of that dead wasted comic thrown-away body strained for air on this one. No air: only hydrocyanic acid gas. Just nerves, like the fish twitching after you whack it on the skull with the back edge of the skinning knife. Except that it wasn't a fish we were seeing die.

His head flopped sideways and his tongue came out slyly like the tongue of a dead deer. Then this gunk ran out of his mouth. It was just saliva—they said it couldn't be anything else—but it reminded me of the residue after light-line resistors have been melted in an electrical fire. That kind of black. That kind of scorched.

Very softly, almost to himself, Victor murmured: "Later, dad."

That was it. Dig you in the hereafter, dad. Ten little minutes and you're thorough the wall. Mistah Kurtz, he dead. Mistah Kurtz, he very very goddamn dead.

I believed it. Looking at what was left of that cat was like looking at a chick who's gotten herself bombed on the heavy, so when you hold a match in front of her eyes the pupils don't react and there's no one home, man. No one. Nowhere. End of the lineville.

We split.

But on the way out I kept thinking of that Army stud, and wondering what had made him sick. Was it because the cat in the chair had been the last to enter, no matter how violently, the body of his beloved, and now even that feeble connection had been severed? Whatever the reason, his body had known what perhaps his mind had refused to accept: this ending was no new beginning, this death would not restore his dead chick to him. This death, no matter how just in his eyes, had generated only nausea.

Victor and I sat in the Mercedes for a long time with the top down, looking out over that bright beautiful empty peninsula, not named, as you might think, after a saint, but after some poor dumb Indian they had hanged there a hundred years or so before. Trees and clouds and blue water, and still no birds making the scene. Even the cats in the black suits had vanished, but now I understood why they'd been there. In their silent censure, they had been sounding the right gong, man. *We* were the ones from the Middle Ages.

Victor took a deep shuddering breath as if he could never get enough air. Then he said in a barely audible voice: "How did you dig that action, man?"

I gave a little shrug and, being myself, said the only thing I could say. "It was a gas, dad."

"I dig, man. I'm hip. A gas."

Something was wrong with the way he said it, but I broke the seal on the tequila and we killed it in fifteen minutes, without even a lime to suck in between. Then he started the car and we cut out, and I realized what was wrong. Watching that cat in the gas chamber, Victor had realized for the very first time that life is far, far more than just kicks. We were both partially responsible for what had happened in there, and we had been ineluctably diminished by it.

On U.S. 101 he coked the Mercedes up to 104 m.p.h. through the traffic, and held it there. It was wild: it was the end: but I didn't sound. I was alone without my Guide by the boiling river of blood. When the Highway Patrol finally stopped us, Victor was coming on so strong and I was coming on so mild that they surrounded us with their holster flaps unbuckled, and checked our veins for needle marks.

I didn't say a word to them, man, not one. Not even my name. Like they had to look in my wallet to see who I was. And while they were doing that, Victor blew his cool entirely. You know, biting, foaming at the mouth, the whole bit—he gave a very good show until they hit him on the back of the head with a gun butt. I just watched.

They lifted his license for a year, nothing else, because his old man spent a lot of bread on a shrinker who testified that Victor had temporarily wigged out, and who had him put away in the zoo for a time. He's back now, but he still sees that wig picker, three times a week at forty clams a shot.

He needs it. A few days ago I saw him on Upper Grant, stalking lithely through a gray raw February day with the fog in, wearing just a T-shirt and jeans—and no shoes. He seemed agitated, pressed, confined within his own concerns, but I stopped him for a minute.

"Ah . . . how you making it, man? Like, ah, what's the gig?"

He shook his head cautiously. "They will not let us get away with it, you know. Like to them, man, just living is a crime."

"Why no strollers, dad?"

"I cannot wear shoes." He moved closer and glanced up and down the street, and said with tragic earnestness: "I can hear only with the soles of my feet, man."

Then he nodded and padded away through the crowds on silent naked soles like a puzzled panther, drifting through the fruiters and drunken teenagers and fuzz trying to bust some cat for possession who have inherited North Beach from the true swingers. I guess all Victor wants to listen to now is Mother Earth: all he wants to hear is the comforting sound of the worms, chewing away.

Chewing away, and waiting for Victor; and maybe for the Second Coming.

I wrote "Raptor" after reading Miyamotu Musashi's Book of Five Rings, *a 17th Century guide for samurais going into battle against evil Warlords. I chose as my hero Dunstan Trevor, a reluctant warrior facing a hitman hired by one of the Warlords of our day, a Mafia don. But Raptor makes his own rules about who, when and how he kills.*

RAPTOR

At eleven p.m., Spiro Gounaris, a hawk-nosed man carrying fifty years and forty extra pounds, locked the door of the second-hand store which fronted his treasury book. He crossed the sidewalk to the phonebooth, as he had done for six nights in a row. As he dropped his dime and tapped out the Federal Prosecutor Task Force number, Raptor came bopping along in shades and a poppy beret—*on my way home from an early gig man.*

Unlike the previous nights, Raptor saw no other pedestrians on the street. Gounaris was saying, "Seven-thousand two-hundred and eighty" into the phone when Raptor pressed the muzzle of the short-barreled .357 Magnum against the back of his head and pulled the trigger. . . .

At three minutes to midnight, Raptor walked into a gas station three miles away and laid five twenties with a note clipped to them on top of the pump the night man was locking up.

"The pay phone," said Raptor.

The phone was saying, "Hello, this is Dunstan Trevis speaking," as the night man, a kid in his twenties, came up tentatively. Raptor handed him the receiver to hear the rest of the message. At the tone, the kid cleared his throat and read from the note, "Uh—this is Raptor. Uh—I gave the gentleman the message. It—uh—really blew his mind."

Dunstan Trevis was a compact man in his thirties, a shade over five-ten and under 170, with tired dispassionate eyes behind bookish hornrims in a cool, uninvolved face. He switched off the phone machine's playback mechanism and walked through the apartment to his bedroom.

How now! A rat? Dead, for a ducat, dead!

He drew a mental line through *Gounaris, S.* on the list he carried in his head. Five dead rats in the two-plus years he'd been controller for Prince Industries. He felt as he always did when there was a message from Raptor on the machine: ready to throw up, yet determined to go on. No one on the Board knew it, but he'd set Gounaris up so that going to the Feds must have seemed the only way out. And so the Board had ordered the hit.

Trevis undressed and got into bed. Only five years before he'd been a computer software designer for United Electrodata, with a brilliant future, a growing portfolio, some very nice stock options, and a wedding date set.

Then Teresa had died.

Out of that terrible time had come his resolve. He started drinking, methodically, destructively. The folio dwindled, the options lapsed, the future disappeared. Once he was far enough down, he dried out, found a bookkeeping job with the Dahlgren subsidiary of Prince Industries, and in two months was head bookkeeper. He was made controller of Prince Industries when they realized he had a remarkable ability to invent new and startling ways to launder illicit cash.

★ ★ ★ ★ ★

Now, Trevis slept.

the dum dum smashed through her skull.

He came up out of it screaming. Sitting on the edge of the bed, he wiped the sweat from his face with a corner of the sheet. Always the same, it never varied—except they were more frequent.

He courted sleep, as usual, with Miyamotu Musashi's BOOK OF FIVE RINGS, the great Seventeenth Century guide for samurai intent on defeating their enemies in battle. But sleep continued to elude him. It wasn't fear of death—too much of him had died with Teresa for that. It was that he had to change the equation. When you cannot see the enemy's spirit, said Musashi, make a feint attack to discover his resources. He will show his long sword, thinking he sees your spirit.

Risk everything in a feint, in hopes of uncovering whoever had been responsible for Teresa's death.

But meanwhile, sleep. One of his functions was to act as the Board's buffer man. Through him people who didn't want to meet while conducting business didn't have to. Hence, he was the buffer between Raptor and the Board. And between the Board and Letterman, their tame cop who had fingered Gounaris to the Board. Tomorrow he had to meet Letterman, and Letterman would be howling.

Lieutenant Jack Letterman of the city's Organized Crime Squad had a hard, lined face and doleful blue eyes tipped down at the outer corners like a bloodhound's. His suit was not quite expensive enough to raise questions about his income. He entered one of Vince O'Neill's porn parlors past the garish yellow and red sign: HOT STUFF—25¢ ARCADE—FANTASY IN FLESH! Covering the walls were intimate photos of women wearing nothing but expressions seldom seen in full daylight. In a raised change-cage, a stout middle-aged woman reading that morning's *Wall Street Journal* said, "The-hottest-show-in-town-have-a-good-time" without looking up from her stock quotations.

Letterman entered the labyrinth of coin machines where mobile masks of light flickered over the features of the male viewers peering into the eyepieces. Perfumed disinfectant gave it a county-jail smell. In the rear was Trevis, showing no slightest interest in what he was seeing. Letterman fed three quarters, good for three minutes, into the machine next to his.

"I didn't expect a hit on Gounaris," he complained. "The boys down at the federal building are really burned. There's going to be too much heat for me to pass anything on for a while. I've got a pension to protect."

Trevis shrugged almost sullenly, handed him a newspaper with his blood money folded inside, and walked out.

Milton Prince was in his mid-fifties, dynamic, corrupt, kept fit by massages, saunas, and heroic avoidance of the pasta he loved. His name had once carried extra syllables—*rhymes with spaghetti* had been the schoolyard taunt of the predominantly Irish kids at St. Paddy's across the river. The syllables had been dropped just about the time some of those erstwhile youthful taunters had started walking funny, or seen their businesses torched, or watched with a gun at their heads while three or four strangers entertained their wives.

"How was the weekend?" he asked Trevis.

Trevis removed his glasses to ponder the question, as he always did. He finally admitted, "I tried the intermediate run for the first time, Mr. Prince."

Prince chuckled. "You? Skiing! I just can't—"

But the time for small talk was past. The glasses had gone back on. Trevis, sorting through his paper-stuffed briefcase, said, "You'll find Raptor's payment on the Gounaris matter under Write-off Against Depreciation on page six of the printout." He paused. "Our friend downtown tells me the Feds were very upset to lose their star informant before they could get him in front of the grand jury."

Prince's eyes sharpened. "How upset is very?"

"Letterman is trying to back away from us."

"And if the Feds find out he's on the pad?"

"He'll get into bed with them." Then, because Letterman, while venal, was not on his mental list, Trevis added, "I recommend *no action* by the Board at this time, Mr. Prince. It would remove the immediate problem but create a long-term one. The police are very stubborn when one of their own is taken."

Not that Trevis expected Prince to follow his recommendation. Prince would do exactly as he wished. Prince was answerable only to the Board, locally.

Uh—this is Raptor," said the cassette player on Prince's desk. Uh—I gave the gentleman the message. It—uh—really blew his mind."

"I got it off Trevis's answering machine yesterday," said Eddie Ucelli. He was a skull-crusher who had worked his way up from union strongarm to made-man to a member of the Board.

"My friend at the police lab voice-printed it," said Otto Kreiger, the firm's corporate counsel and also on the Board. "Another different voice—just like all the others."

Raptor doesn't make mistakes," said Prince in admiration. "He doesn't give us a handle on him."

Nearly three years earlier, the Board had determined to put out a contract on Christiansen, who was getting too ambitious, but before they could a man named Raptor hit him—for free. A sample of his work. Since then, he had carried out four other impeccable internal eliminations for the Board, but they knew absolutely nothing about him. From the first he had insisted on a buffer man and a series of mail cut-outs beyond the buffer. The Board had chosen Trevis as buffer man, and it seemed a safe arrangement. But they still kept trying to find out about Raptor, just for insurance.

Ucelli tossed a newspaper clipping on the desk. "I thought I'd snoop Trevis's desk while I was there, and I found this. Maybe it don't mean nothing, it's five or six years old, but she used to work for the Dahlgren subsidiary—"

A woman named Teresa Bianca had been shot and killed instantly in a downtown bar by an unknown assailant who escaped into the Christmas-shopper crowds. One of the dozen listed witnesses was a Dunstan Trevis.

"I remember the case," said Kreiger. "A very professional seeming hit. But the Board never ordered—"

Prince was nodding. "Not one of ours." He shrugged and crumpled up the clipping, tossing it into the wastebasket.

But after the other two had gone, Prince recovered it and smoothed it out on his desk blotter. His shirt was suddenly stuck to his back. Teresa Bianca, Whittington's secretary and a snoopy little broad. No, the Board hadn't ordered the hit on her. It hadn't ordered the hit on Whittington either, but he'd been lucky because everyone bought that as an accident, pure and simple.

Put Driscoll on Trevis, that was it. Driscoll was a small-time private eye owned by Prince. Nothing would get back to the Board from Driscoll, but Driscoll could find out if there was anything to worry about with Trevis. Meanwhile, just for his own peace of mind, he wanted to find a way around Trevis to Raptor, direct, without anyone else on the Board knowing about it. To do that he would have to call a Board on Letterman.

It was a full Board, very formal and full of all that man-of-respect drool they had picked up from THE GODFATHER. Held in the executive boardroom, because who wanted to meet in a drafty warehouse or upstairs over a pizza joint when this was comfortable and secure? Prince, as capo, presided. Around the table were the men who controlled shylocking, porn, whores, drugs, garbage, linen, jukeboxes, trucking, and gambling in the city and the southern half of the state.

"Mr. Ucelli is recommending a contract be let on Lieutenant Letterman," said Prince. "Our buffer man, Mr. Trevis, opposes such action at this time."

Trevis, not being a member of the Board, was not present, of course, but his view had its adherents. Gideon Abramson, loan shark and a grandfather eight times over, said, "There is a great deal of heat over this Gounaris thing. The Feds have so many people on the street my collectors keep tripping over them. To hit an Organized Crime Squad cop at this time—"

"He talks, he can hurt us bad," objected Spignola, garbage and linen.

"Who? Who can he take down?" Friedman's street-drug sales were being curtailed by the federal heat. "The buffer man? Trevis? Big deal. Mr. Nobody, am I not right?"

Prince, who was worried by the possibility that he wasn't

49

right, waited while Kreiger made the point that Raptor might not want to hit someone outside the organization itself, then said smoothly, "I believe it should be put to a vote. All those in favor so indicate." And he raised his own hand.

Following the Board's directive, Dunstan Trevis typed *Mr. Porter Edwards, Edwards' Tow Truck and Wrecking Service, 4853 Harbor Drive* on a six-by-nine manila clasp envelope with first-class postage already affixed. In this he put a small sealed unaddressed white envelope containing a three-by-five index card on which he had typed:

Jack Letterman

accident

As always, he was using one of the public typewriters in the third-floor stacks of the public library. As he stood up, a young woman with an armload of books ran into him. Her books flew in every direction. She seemed to be in her early twenties and wore no bra under her see-through blouse.

"I'm really sorry," she said in a flustered voice, retrieving his fallen envelope as he picked up her books.

He assured her it was all right and departed to mail the envelope. The girl, who was actually a woman in her thirties, dumped her books on the floor and dictated the Porter Edwards address into her micro-mini cassette recorder before she forgot any of it. That night, well after dark, her employer Larry Driscoll delivered the cassette to Milton Prince.

Jack Letterman was two-fingering a report while trying to remember if counselor—as in attorney—had one "l" or two when the phone rang. Picking up and barking, "Crime

Squad, Letterman," he heard the high-pitched, high-speed delivery of Burkie, one of his snitches, which could be stemmed only by interruptions.

"This one'll cost you, sweetheart, it's hot, in writing. You can use it to cool out the Feds if they come down on you—"

"The usual place?"

"Yeah, the door's sticking, you gotta almost kick it—"

"Fifteen minutes."

Letterman checked out a car and drove to Burkie's latest drop, another deserted tenement. Burkie was just a voice on the phone who had started selling Letterman information about a year and a half before. For the first few times Letterman had gone into the condemned buildings in a rush, with his piece drawn, but there was never anything except envelopes of incredibly good intelligence for which he left envelopes of cash and which he peddled to the Feds and the wise guys with even-handed impartiality.

Letterman huffed up the narrow exterior back stairs to the third-floor landing, where he rammed the sticking door with his shoulder when it refused to open.

Tiny flames spurted from the kitchen matchheads stuck between the edge of the door and the thin strip of flint paper fixed to the frame. With a whoosh, gas from the ruptured line just inside the door ignited.

The explosion rocked the deserted building. Raptor, wearing a repairman's bulky overalls and a flowing bandido mustache, had to duck back into the ground-floor rear entryway across the alley to avoid being hit by part of Letterman. He was boarding a city bus two blocks away when the first police and fire units arrived on the scene.

I was working late, clearing my desk, and Mr. Whittington left with this man. An hour later he was dead. They're saying it was an accident, but, Dun, I don't believe that. And now I'm afraid there's someone following me. . . .

He laughed at her fears.

And he was late for their Christmas-shopping excursion.

Walking into the bar, he saw her welcoming smile, but then the man who'd walked in ahead of him shot her once in the head from a foot away. It was such a heavy caliber the man's arm flew a foot into the air with the recoil.

Someone is following me. I'm frightened. Help me, darling.

He'd actually laughed.

She'd actually died.

Trevis came awake, hearing the slug enter her brain, feeling it bulge her laughing eyes. He read Musashi. Musashi said: Become the enemy. Musashi said: The enemy, shut up inside his own spirit, is a pheasant. You, becoming him, are a hawk. Consider this deeply, Musashi said.

Prince paced. He absently put down Driscoll's reports, and paced. It was raining; water streamed down the outside of his study windows. Nobody had ever turned up Trevis's connection with the Bianca broad because until Driscoll's sieve job nobody had looked.

Prince built himself a strong drink and paced the sumptuous study while he sipped it. The shape of it all was easy to see, now he had the facts. Six years before, he'd gotten in deep and had had to start skimming—using Whittington, bookkeeper of the Dahlgren subsidiary. But Whittington had gotten scared. If he'd talked, the Board would have canceled Prince's ticket, so Whittington had to go. But then his secretary, Teresa Bianca, got suspicious, so she had to go, too. Afterward, the whole thing seemed to have blown over.

But she must have told things to Trevis before she was

hit. So he turned into a drunk just so he could get fired from where he worked and then sober up and get himself hired by the Dahlgren subsidiary. And then, as he was using his brilliance to burrow into the guts of the organization, trying to find out who had ordered the hit, the Board had made him buffer man and had given him Raptor, the ultimate killing machine. He didn't have to dig any more. He just had to start setting up the men who'd been on the Board when she was killed, one after the other, using Raptor as a personal hit man. And he'd just keep on manufacturing evidence and having Board members killed until he reached Milton Prince anyway. By accident.

Only now it wasn't going to happen. Because now Prince could reach the killing machine without putting Trevis's finger on the trigger. He sat down to compose his letter to Raptor.

Porter Edwards was a big easygoing black who ran a one-truck tow service from his junk yard on the mud flats near the river. As he tore open the six-by-nine manila envelope to remove the smaller white envelope, he felt not the slightest curiosity about what was inside. He got twelve hundred bucks a year to not be curious. That money had kept the truck running lots of times, and had paid for the birthing of their fourth child. He wrote a name and address on a manila envelope just like the one he had torn open, and posted it.

The sign said CISCO'S TEXAS TACOS. Cisco shoved the small sealed unaddressed white envelope into a new six-by-nine manila and remembered. Three years ago, three-thirty in the morning, the place deserted and the door open to let out the hot grease smell of deep-frying taco shells as he swept up. A man dressed in black, with black gloves, and wearing a Porky Pig Halloween mask, had come in and taken a stool. Then he had taken a gun with a silencer screwed onto it out of his pocket. His voice had been distorted by the mask.

"Are you interested in a hundred dollars a month, payable twice yearly?"

Cisco, transfixed by the silenced muzzle, managed to say, "Yes."

"I thought you would be." And Porky Pig had put the gun away.

The squat man tried to kick Tommy Yet in the stomach. Tommy blocked the kick outward with his left forearm, simultaneously countering with a right forward kick which would have ruptured his opponent if Tommy hadn't stopped it two millimeters short.

They dropped their arms and bowed. The students clapped.

Tommy Yet was a slight, compact man who could break bones and mangle flesh, smash bricks with his fists, knock down walls with his feet. He also was a Zen Buddhist who revered all life and dealt, not in violence, but in discipline and control.

Unfortunately, three years before, his daughter Perching Bird—named after one of the stylized movements of the Great Circle—had been born with pyloric stenosis. This narrowing of the stomach, which prevented the ingestion of any food, cost ten thousand dollars to correct surgically. When Tommy couldn't keep up on the loan shark's three-for-two vigorish, men came around to tell him what they were going to do with his wife and child the following week if he didn't pay them.

Tommy cast the Ching, which confirmed that he must kill them upon their return, and then kill himself to wash away the stain of the dishonor. But an hour before they showed up, a man walked in with fifteen thousand dollars in cash for the loan shark. All he asked in return was that Tommy forward to a certain post-office box any mail that might come for him.

Tommy never saw the man again.

He locked up the dojo and went out to the car when his wife honked the horn. He asked her to stop at a mailbox on the way home so he could drop in a six-by-nine manila envelope.

At one fifty-four a.m., Raptor leaned forward and thrust a twenty-dollar bill and a long-shanked brass post-office key to the driver through the plexiglass partition which had on it, *Thank You for Not Smoking in My Cab.* The box to which Tommy Yet had mailed the manila envelope had an automatic forwarding on it to this box. There was a message waiting from Milton Prince.

Our firm now wishes to deal with you direct, as we are terminating the services of our controller as soon as possible. Your rate of renumeration is doubled, effective immediately.

Please advise acceptance through a classified personal ad in the morning newspaper, to Worried from R.

Prince read it in the newspaper a week later.

Worried:
His ski lodge, Saturday night, seven.
R.

Trevis left the office at one-thirty Saturday afternoon with his usual bulging briefcase and trudged across the deserted acre of blacktop company parking lot to find Mr. Prince waiting in the front seat of his two-year-old Datsun hatchback. Prince was wearing heavy clothes and hiking boots.

"I want to go up to that ski lodge of yours, Dunstan."

Trevis was silent for a few moments. "Well, to tell you the truth, Mr. Prince, it's more a shack than a—"

"I came prepared," said Prince jovially and gestured at the pile of equipment in the back of the Datsun. He dropped his voice and leaned closer. "I want to talk to you about something I don't want the rest of the Board to know."

When they reached the snowline, where the sleet of lower elevations turned to large wet flakes that hit the windshield and slid down, Prince was still talking.

"In the last few years five of our top people—members of the Board—had to go because they put self-interest ahead of their commitment to the organization. So I need someone at the Board meetings I can trust—someone logical, who understands business practices."

Trevis pulled off onto the shoulder of the road just beyond a flip-down sign which read, CHAINS REQUIRED BEYOND THIS POINT.

"I'm not a made-man," he pointed out.

"There's a way around that. If I can get national approval to expand into the northern half of the state we'll *have* to fill Gounaris's empty seat on the Board. I want you to have that seat, Dunstan."

He sat in the car, soaking up the heater warmth, as Trevis moved around outside fixing the chains through the thickly falling flakes. That notion of expanding, that was actually a hell of a good idea. Maybe after Trevis was eliminated he'd fly down to the Bahamas, get some sun, put out a few cautious feelers with Bruno as to how the national organization would react to such a move.

After Trevis had got back in, bringing icy air with him, Prince listened to the chains thump in their even, hypnotic rhythm, and wondered how Raptor would do it. This one, he knew, he wanted to watch.

The cabin was a big central room with a couple of little bedrooms partitioned off, and a tiny kitchen in back with a three-burner kerosene stove. Prince wandered around looking at the pictures on the walls with his hands in the pockets of his fancy new down jacket while Trevis got the fire started. The photos were of skiers, hunters, fishermen, and hikers who had used this place and seemed to enjoy it, all grins and rough clothes.

As the iron potbellied wood stove started to take the chill off the room, Trevis pumped up the kerosene pressure lamp until the double mantles glowed white-hot.

"I'll close the shades," said Prince. "They'll keep the heat in."

He went from window to window, pulling down the cheap roller shades and staring out through the cold glass of each window. It was two minutes to seven.

Are you out there waiting somewhere, Raptor? Are you ready, Raptor?

Raptor checked the luminous face of his watch.

6:59:01 and :02 and :03. . . .

It was time.

Trevis heaved his bulging briefcase up on the table and

opened it. "I've got some printouts here, Mr. Prince, that might suggest some avenues initiating expansion."

Prince stopped him with a wave of the hand. He had an unpleasant smile on his face. "You won't need those, Trevis. I've had a full report on you and Teresa Bianca. I know what you've been doing these past three years." He chuckled. "You've finally found the man you've been looking for."

Trevis slowly let the papers he had started to bring out slide back in the case. His face was very white.

"I used the Letterman hit to bypass you, Trevis. Raptor is going to kill you. Here. Tonight. Right now."

As he spoke, Trevis's eyes shifted beyond him to the door. His eyes widened.

Prince looked at the door, almost feeling the icy blast from outside. The door was still closed. He turned back to see Trevis's right hand come out of the briefcase holding a Walther MPK machine pistol. The muzzle of the Walther, extended by a gas cylinder silencer, was pointed at Prince.

"I couldn't stomach any more random killing, Prince, so I put that newspaper clipping where Ucelli would find it. I hoped it would bring whoever I was after out into the open." He paused. "I'm Raptor."

Prince's face felt suddenly bloodless. His mouth was without saliva. He thrust out his hands, palms forward. "Money . . ."

The silenced sub-machinegun made a series of earnest busy clicking sounds. Blood and bone leaped from the front of Prince's head. Splinters and chips flew from the wall behind him. The gun followed him down, clicking and chattering to itself until the magazine was empty.

Raptor stood for a long moment with the machine pistol hanging straight down at his side. Even an excised tumor leaves a feeling of loss.

Trevis returned the gun to the briefcase, shut it, and with his gloved left hand turned the pump on the lantern. There was the hiss of escaping pressure. By the mantles' dying glow, he picked his way across the unfamiliar room he'd rented by phone, in Prince's name, earlier in the week, and had paid for with a cashier's check. He had never been skiing in his life.

Outside, the snow had stopped. Stars crowded the black sky. A nice night for a drive down the mountain. Then he thought: To what? Wasn't he by this time so steeped in blood that—

But then, in a sudden blinding moment of insight, he understood the ultimate truth in Miyamotu Musashi's book which had eluded him until now. The Fifth Ring, said Musashi, was the final strategy. The Fifth Ring was the way of the Void. In the Void was only virtue, without evil.

Raptor was in the Void. Raptor was of the Void.

Two men had died back there in the cabin.

Trevis was now free of both of them.

I had just written a script for a half-hour TV drama series (to be narrated by Orson Wells) that had died aborning, when a Japanese magazine asked me for a story. I changed unused script into story, giving Wells' narrative voice to the unknown murderer of an unpleasant attorney in my only locked-room tale to date.

PLOT IT YOURSELF

Wasn't it Shakespeare who suggested that we kill all the lawyers? Too drastic? Well, then, what about *one* lawyer?

I am his murderer.

Can you catch me?

I won't lie to you. Oh, I might *tease* you a little. Do a bit of business over here with my left hand to hold your eye, say, while over here my right hand is doing, oh, maybe, murder.

A widely held misconception is that Beverly Hills is inhabited by movie folk. But only eight percent of the mansions on those wide, shady, deserted streets, drowsy with the swish of automatic sprinklers and the clip-clip of hedge shears, are owned by the Sly Stallones and the Jane Fondas. In the rest live doctors and dentists and psychiatrists and attorneys and clothes-hanger manufacturers and Rolls Royce salesmen.

Take that white mansion with stately southern pillars set well back from Beverly Glen on an acre of lawn. It houses— pardon me, *housed*—an entertainment law attorney named Eric Stalker. On the night of his murder, streetlights were going on as Stalker parked his Lagonda (one of twenty-four imported into the U.S. that year) behind a white Continental, a midnight-blue Rolls, and his stepdaughter's red bat-wing Mercedes coupe.

Stalker was a handsome, gray-haired, vital fifty-six, with the tanning-salon's all-over mahogany skin color and the spring to his step that only hours in the gym can give. As he closed the car door—a solid, monied clunk—an eight-year-old Chev Nova, with one fender a different color from the rest, crunched to a stop on the gravel drive behind the Lagonda.

Chuck Hoffe fit his machine: early thirties, tough-looking, mean of face and cold of eye, wearing the sort of off-the-rack suit associated in the popular mind with the honest cop.

"Chuck—you don't mind if I call you Chuck, do you? I'm delighted that you—"

Hoffe shook Stalker's arm off his shoulder almost testily. "If you invited me here tonight hoping I'll change my testimony tomorrow—"

Stalker shifted his slim attaché case to emphasize it. "Let's go to my study before we join the others, Chuck. I have something in here that you'll find intriguing."

Eric Stalker, leading this vice cop off toward the French doors to his study, is playing a dangerous game with Hoffe and with his other guests now congregating in the dining room. Did I say dangerous? Deadly, rather. Because, as Dickens once pointed out, if there were no bad people, there would be no good lawyers. Stalker is a *very* good lawyer. And his guests—well, they're the sort of people who *need* very good lawyers.

It was a small formal dining room, the walls covered by

Thirteenth Century tapestries depicting the cardinal sin of gluttony with all the hypocritically self-indulgent detail so beloved of the medieval artist. The chandelier was Czecho-slovakian crystal and the flatware so solidly silver that the forks could be easily bent by hand if one were so gauche as to do so.

No nouvelle cuisine here: shad roe *aux fines herbes,* a duckling in Flemish olive sauce, and pork fillets braised in a nice spiced Burgundy, served with polenta. They had lingered over the fig-and-cherry tart. Stalker finally rose and tapped his water glass with his knife. Conversation ceased abruptly.

"Yes, of course. You each know why you're here, don't you?" He began walking slowly down the length of the table behind their chairs, all eyes moving with him. "I hinted—"

He stopped behind his stepdaughter, Merrilee, a sensual, spoiled-looking woman in her early twenties, not at all beautiful but with an obviously very bedable look about her. As he leaned over to speak above her, she stared straight ahead, a sullen expression on her face.

"Right, Merrilee? I no more than *hinted*—"

"Yes, Father. Only hinted."

He paused behind Jon Norliss, a distinguished, white-haired man of about seventy who was lighting a cigar as if at peace with himself and the world. He seemed indifferent to Stalker's face beaming over his shoulder.

"Yes. Hinted that I might *give* each of you something."

Norliss nodded, turning his cigar to get it burning evenly. Stalker nodded also, and moved on to Andy Bowman, an obvious health addict in his mid-forties, with a handsome face and an assured, slightly sardonic air.

"Something that you want very much." Stalker's voice suddenly snapped. "Isn't that so, Andy?"

"Yes, Eric," said Bowman evenly.

Stalker had passed around the end of the table to Chuck Hoffe's place. The plainclothesman was half turned to watch him.

"I have thought each of your situations over very carefully indeed," said Stalker. "And I have decided that I'm not giving any of you one damned thing."

He nodded, beaming, and slipped out of the room through the door behind him. Hoffe already was halfway to his feet, his face contorted, exclaiming, "I could kill you for this, Stalker!"

All of them, stunned, were on their feet by this time, crowding through the doorway after Stalker.

"You promised me!"

"I was led to believe—"

"Your own daughter, you couldn't—"

But Stalker stepped into his study and closed the door behind him. They heard the bolt being shot home. Hoffe strode angrily to the massive front door, face set and eyes murderous.

What was it The Saint used to say Chief Inspector Teal from Scotland Yard was being afflicted with? Detectivitis, I believe. I can see you sharpening your wits for the challenge I am setting you, my friend. Beware of detectivitis—what is needed here is *observation*. Watch closely now. No detail is too miniscule to be unimportant. Don't let your eyes deceive you.

Stalker paused to grin at himself and fuss with his carnation in the ornate full-length mirror fastened to the back of the door. Then he crossed the thick oriental carpet to a painting beside the French doors behind his desk. He swung the hinged painting back against the wall and worked the combination of the safe it concealed. After opening the safe door against the back of the painting, he left it that way, taking nothing from it.

He sat down in the heavy leather swivel chair behind his desk and surveyed the room with a self-satisfied look on his face. He was quite alone. He took paper and an envelope from the top side drawer and began writing with an old-fashioned inkwell pen. The pen made scratching sounds in the silence of the study.

I told you I wouldn't deceive you, so we will take a quick peek at the rest of the characters in our little drama as Stalker writes his rather nasty screed in his locked study.

Stepdaughter Merrilee is at the makeup table in her room on the second floor, shredding a handkerchief with her teeth and cursing her stepfather. She abruptly gets to her feet and starts for the door with great resolve.

Stalker's partner in the law office, courtly looking Jon Norliss, is out in back by the pool, pausing to knock the ash off his cigar. He loses control, shreds it against the retaining wall. Now he is turning determinedly back toward the house.

Stalker's Beverly Hills physician, the dashing Andy Bowman, is throwing up into the toilet on the second floor. He suffers a spastic stomach in moments of ultimate decision.

The vice-cop, Chuck Hoffe, has been walking in circles on the front lawn, smoking a cigarette down to the filter. He throws it away with sudden resolution and strides rapidly off.

Detectivitis, anyone?

Stalker looked up into the face of the person in the

middle of the room. In that frozen moment of realization, he could see himself exactly as that person saw him.

A handsome, distinguished man, old-fashioned pen in his left hand, inkwell open on the upper-left-hand corner of the desk blotter. Behind him, the painting swung back against the wall to the right of the wall safe it usually concealed, with the safe door still open against the back of the painting. To the left of the opened safe were the French doors, drapes closed, door latched.

After a moment, as if there were no one else in the room with him, he turned over the sheet of foolscap to blot it, then folded it into the envelope. As he wrote on the envelope, he looked up into that face again.

"You can't possibly think you're going to get away with this, you know," he said in a voice which strove for lightness.

There was no response. Was that perhaps a flicker of fear in Stalker's eyes? He licked the envelope and put it in the desk, his hands resting on the edge of the still-open drawer.

"Take some time to reconsider?" he asked almost hopefully.

There was no response.

He shouted, "All right, then, damn you, get it ov—"

There was a single gunshot, shockingly loud in the enclosed room. Stalker was slammed backward against his chair by the blast, his arms flying wide with its force.

A smoking .357 Magnum thudded to the carpet several feet from the desk. Stalker was tipped back as if sleeping, legs splayed out under the desk, arms hanging laxly outside the arms of the chair. Red had blossomed on his shirt-front.

A silhouette loomed up against the French doors. Cupped hands circled a face pressed against the glass as the person outside tried to peer in through the closed curtains. The latch rattled, but held.

From beyond the bolted door of the study came confused sounds, muffled voices. Someone began beating on the door, then a key was turned in the lock. The knob was turned, rattled. The door would not open. The bolt held.

From the French doors came the sound of breaking glass.

In the hallway, Merrilee was still trying her key in the lock when the bolt was drawn from the inside. Bowman was crowding her shoulder as the door swung in to frame Chuck Hoffe and Jon Norliss in the opening.

"Stalker's dead," Hoffe said matter-of-factly.

Merrilee and Bowman shoved past him into the room without speaking, to get a glimpse of the body slumped behind the desk.

Ah, yes, my friend, these are the vital moments for the little gray cells, as Hercule Poirot was fond of calling them. Everything is laid bare for the inquiring mind that wants to know. Remember, there are only the study door and the French doors. Remember, also, that everyone is suspect.

"Look—don't touch," warned Hoffe. "I have to call forensics. But before I do—"

He stood on the other side of the desk from the dead man, the others ranging naturally behind him. He pointed as he spoke. "Just so we agree on the physical evidence. Stalker is slumped in his chair behind his desk, dead, shot once through the old pump. Powder burns around the wound. The inkwell on the upper-right corner of the desk has been overturned and the ink has spilled out. A .357 Magnum is lying on the floor approximately ten feet from the right edge of the desk. It is probably the murder weapon, probably dropped there by the killer. Okay so far?"

There were several assenting sounds. He went on.

"On the wall behind the desk is a hinged painting, swung open so it is lying against the wall to the left of a wall safe, which is also open. To the right of the safe, the French doors are now open. One pane is broken and glass is shattered inward across the floor. Those doors were locked when I tried them from the outside—I had to bust one of the panes to get in."

No reactions. Hoffe wrapped a handkerchief around his hand to pick up the phone receiver. He tapped out a number. "Since we've agreed on the crime scene, I'll call it in."

No one dissented. Bowman, ever the physician, crouched beside the body to check the obviously dead wrist for a pulse. Norliss stared glumly at the body.

Bowman stood up and shrugged. "The Grim Reaper and all that."

"Vengeance is mine, saith the Lord," intoned Norliss.

"Vengeance is a .357 Magnum slug through the heart," said Hoffe, coming up beside them.

"Stop this! All of you!" cried Merrilee suddenly. They turned to look at her in surprise. There were tears in her eyes. "Sarcasm and platitudes when—when my father is *dead. Murdered!*" She turned suddenly on Hoffe. "And *you* just said, a few minutes ago, that you were going to kill him."

For just an instant, Hoffe looked guilty, then his normal brash, cocky manner reasserted itself. He started striding up and down the carpet beside the desk, gesturing as he did.

"Sure, I'll admit I was steamed. That's why I went out to smoke a cigarette, to get control of myself. But then I heard this shot. I ran back, tried the French doors—they were locked, as I said. I looked through the curtains and saw him here—dead. So I—"

"You could have opened those doors earlier!" cried Merrilee.

"I didn't like him any better than the rest of you," said Hoffe patiently, "but why would I kill him?"

At that moment, a strange voice said, "Raoul, I want you to put your hand on her shoulder."

See everyone look in different directions? Now look at the twenty-nine inch screen of the floor-model TV console in the corner. Yes, a pornographic film now flickers there! A bedroom with a handsome naked man in bed with a naked blonde girl who doesn't look out of her teens. Might not this be a clue?

The man put his hand on the girl's shoulder. The unknown voice said, "Turn her toward you—"

There was a loud click and the screen went blank. Hoffe had pushed past Bowman to the video-machine controls.

"I think we should see the rest of it," said Bowman. "A porn flick—and Mr. Hoffe here is a vice cop."

Hoffe, meeting nothing but stony dislike in any eye, stepped back with a shrug. "All right," he said, "show the damned thing. See what it gets you."

The porn movie flickered back on. But this time, as the man reached again for the naked girl, the director's voice burst in, "Who the hell *is* this clown? Somebody get him out of here!"

The camera slewed wildly around the empty warehouse with the bedroom set and lights clustered in the middle of it, then focused on Hoffe and the young vulpine-looking director.

"She's underage, baby," Hoffe said, flashing his tin. "In

this state, seventeen'll get you twenty."

"*Take five, everybody!*" yelled the director. In a stricken undertone to Hoffe, he added, "Hey, man, gimme a break!"

The camera maintained follow focus as they moved away from the set. The director took a roll of bills from his pocket.

"I can beat this thing in court—the girl's older than she looks. But our production deadlines would suffer. I wouldn't want you to lose by not making an arrest—"

Hoffe clicked the machine off again. "That's when I busted him. So you see, Stalker didn't have any knives sticking in me."

"He told me he was going to force you to change your testimony in court tomorrow on this case," said Bowman. After a beat, in an almost admiring voice, he added, "Our Eric was good at things like that."

Hoffe sneered. "Not this time. I have this guy cold."

But the porn scene flashed back on—Bowman's work. "Oh, I won't lose." Hoffe pocketed the roll of money, *then* clapped cuffs on the startled director. "Because you're under arrest, pal, for making pornographic films with an underage girl."

The screen went to snow, then blank. Hoffe sneered at the distaste in their faces.

"Okay, so Stalker had me over a barrel with this film and made me promise in writing to change my testimony to-morrow. He said he'd give me the tape after supper, but—"

"But he didn't and you killed him," said Merrilee.

"Except the tape is still here, girlie!" sneered Hoffe. "Would I kill him and then not take it? Hell, no! This was a grudge job." He turned suddenly. "And *you* had a hell of a grudge against him."

Norliss, caught off-guard, wet suddenly dry lips. He

stammered, "That's nonsense. I don't know what you might have heard, but that disagreement in his office was just business."

Bowman, still crouched in front of the VCR machine to check the tape cabinet beneath it, had taken out Hoffe's tape and inserted another. He pushed the PLAY button and stood up. "Maybe this will tell us what kind of business."

On the TV monitor flashed Stalker's office, taken from a hidden camera. Stalker was behind his desk, dictating a memo. The sound quality was excellent.

"He wired his own office!" gasped Norliss.

The door burst open and Norliss stormed in. He stopped in front of his partner's desk.

"I arrived this morning and found my name removed from my door! I'm going to tell the Bar Association and—"

"Tell them about the Gorsuch case?" asked Stalker silkily.

"I—I don't know what you mean."

Stalker was on his feet, towering over the older, frailer man. "I don't mind your suborning witnesses, Jon, but when you do it so clumsily that I have to spend a great deal of money to get back the evidence and save the firm's name, well—"

"But, Eric, you're the one who demanded I offer—"

"Just sign this letter of resignation, Jon, and I'll turn over the evidence to you. Otherwise—"

The screen went to snow.

I believe it was Cervantes who said that the only comfort of the miserable is to have partners in their woes. But Jon Norliss found small comfort with his partner here tonight. I'm sure he expected to get back the evidence at dinner, and when he learned that he wasn't going to, well, perhaps he—

But there, I'm displaying a touch of detectivitis myself!

Bowman chuckled and shook his head as he took the tape back out of the VCR. "So Eric stiffed you, too, Jon. Just like he did Hoffe. Had you sign the resignation, then kept the evidence against you. So typical. But—"

"What about you?" Norliss burst in angrily. "Your motive for wanting him dead was better than mine. He could have taken my past—but he planned to take *your* future."

Bowman swept an angry hand across the tape titles in the cabinet. "Where's the tape with my name on it, then?"

Before Norliss could answer, Hoffe shot a hand into Bowman's inside coat pocket and yanked out a video tape.

"Right here," he said, shoving Bowman roughly aside.

In a moment, Stalker's office again came up on the screen. Now it was Bowman and the attorney facing each other across the familiar desk, seen from the familiar angle.

"I've decided not to invest in your clinic, after all, Andy," said Stalker in an almost indifferent voice.

Bowman's face crumpled.

"But—but, I—If you don't give me the money—I pledged *everything,* my home, my—"

"I've just found out there was nothing wrong with my gall bladder that a change of diet wouldn't have cured. But *you*—"

Bowman was pleading now. "Eric, please! Maybe the operation *was* marginal, but—but in checking the X-rays afterward I found a—a shadow on your lung. I'm not a specialist in that field, but it could be—"

"Malignant?" Stalker laughed coarsely. "You'd say anything to save the clinic, wouldn't you? Well, crawl for me, Andy. Convince me. If you do, next week, maybe—just maybe . . ."

* * * * *

I think it was an ancient Roman who said it was better to use medicine at the outset than at the last moment. Poor Dr. Bowman! All those financial ills, and he went to Stalker for his medicine. And what did he get for his troubles? Being prime suspect in a murder case. Unless you believe him, of course.

Bowman was clutching his video tape anxiously to his chest. He gave what he thought was a little laugh. "Oh, Eric liked to make people sweat, sure, but I *know* he was going to back my clinic." When nobody spoke, he went on, "If he *did* have cancer, he would have died in a few months. I'd have been a fool to risk a murder charge just so all his money would go to—*her*."

His voice and gesture directed all eyes to Merrilee. They found her using the mirror on the back of the door to freshen her lipstick. She caught their reflection in the glass and laughed.

"Me? Kill Daddy? I *loved* him!" She turned to face them, a sneer on her full lips. "I don't *need* Daddy's money. I have the trust fund my mother left me."

"Administered by Eric!" exclaimed Norliss. "He had full discretion to revoke the trust, and just last week he told me he was drawing up papers to that effect—to sign tomorrow."

"And when I came down from the second floor," exclaimed Bowman, "she was right beside that door, with the key in her hand. She said she heard a shot, and I believed her. "But—"

"Well, well, well," interrupted Hoffe softly. "The little stepdaughter had motive, means, and opportunity—the classic big three for premeditated murder."

Merrilee had paled. She whirled back to the mirror and

pressed her face against it, making a double image of herself. "Stop it," she cried, "all of you! I *did* hear a shot, just like I said! And I heard Daddy in here talking with someone, but I couldn't hear the words." She faced them again, pale features contorted. "You can't *prove* that Daddy planned to—"

She stopped, mouth gaping, as Eric Stalker's rich, sardonic tones filled the room. "A tender—if drunken—scene."

They looked at the corpse, then at the TV. Merrilee's bed was wide, opulent, with a trail of scattered masculine and feminine garments leading to it across the floor. On it, two naked people were leaping guiltily apart.

"The tape was in the safe," explained Hoffe from the VCR machine. "He had his own kid's room wired for pictures."

"Stepkid's," corrected Bowman almost lasciviously.

On the screen, boy and woman had gotten tangled up in each other and the black satin top-sheet had fallen on the floor beside the bed. Stalker entered the frame.

"You—out."

The boy scrambled to his feet "Hey, old man, I ain't scared of you!"

"You should be. Now get out before I—"

"Jerry, do what he says," said the film Merrilee.

"Stop it!" shrieked the real Merrilee.

"*We've* gone through it," said Hoffe. "Now it's your turn."

On the screen, the boy stormed out with his clothes, slamming the door behind him. Stalker was staring at Merrilee as she hastily pulled on a robe over her nakedness.

"I'm cutting off your allowance, Merrilee."

She tried to embrace him, fawning. "Daddy, I'm sorry. I don't know what came over me. I had too much to drink and—you can't!"

He shook her off. "I can and will. It was important to your mother that you be a decent person. I'll revoke the trust if that's what it takes to—"

Merrilee slammed her hand down on the VCR controls and the screen went blank. She turned to glare at the others. "All *right,* he'd taken my allowance and was threatening to revoke the trust. But he promised that if I straightened up he'd give it all back to me!"

"But tonight at dinner he told all of us that he wasn't giving us one damned thing," said Hoffe.

"It could have been any one of us," breathed Norliss.

"Or all of us," said Bowman.

"Sure—or none of us," Merrilee added sarcastically.

Hoffe merely laughed.

What was it that Holmes told Watson? That when you have eliminated the impossible, whatever remains, however improbable, must be the truth? Of course, our suspects' stories should have told you who I, the murderer, am—as well as why I did it. But if you're *still* confused, remember those three classic elements of premeditated murder: motive, means, and opportunity.

"What are you laughing at?" snapped Bowman.

"You all act like this is one of those board games," said Hoffe. "Colonel Mustard in the kitchen with a noose. But this is *real* murder, not—"

"Do you know who did it?" demanded Norliss.

"I'm a detective, aren't I?"

"The police will be here any minute."

"I didn't call them yet. No use going down unnecessarily."

"For—murder?"

"Nah, little girl—for taking a bribe. As for murder—" Hoffe began pacing beside the desk again. Their eyes followed him. "Was it Hoffe, the corrupt cop? No, I had to smash the French doors to get in here and Norliss was with me when I did. Which takes care of him, too. We alibi each other."

Bowman broke in. "If you're saying it was me—"

"You couldn't profit from his murder—you'd still be ruined. And why give him a quick and easy death when he might face a long and lingering one? Besides, Merrilee was at the study door when you came downstairs."

Heads swiveled back to Merrilee, cowering against the now silent TV.

"Merrilee, the disaffected stepdaughter," said Hoffe. "Motive, means, opportunity. Even had a key to get in here." He grinned. "But the door was bolted on the inside, her key couldn't do her any good. It's just like she said. How'd she put it? 'Or none of us?' Yeah. Or none of us."

"But—but there wasn't anyone else," Norliss said.

"Sure, there was," Hoffe told him. Stalker blew himself away."

But you knew I was the killer all the time, didn't you? Because I was the only person who could have done it, from the moment I shot the bolt on that door. I *warned* you that no one could be eliminated as a suspect.

Who was I talking to just before I died? Why, to my own image in the mirror on the back of the door, of course. I even saw myself and the room reversed, if you will remember—pen in my left hand, inkwell on the left corner of the blotter, the picture and the safe door open to the right-hand side, the French doors to the left of the safe.

Hoffe, in repeating the scene after they broke in, listed each item in its proper place. The gun was ten feet from the desk—where my involuntary death spasm threw it. That spasm knocked over the inkwell. There were powder burns because I put the muzzle against my chest before I pulled the trigger.

Yes, I committed the perfect crime.

"Almost," said Hoffe. He was holding the sheet of paper on which Stalker had been writing just before his death. On the opened envelope was written: *To be opened one year after my death.* "Lucky I don't believe in dying wishes," he added. Then he read aloud from the letter:

" 'To whom it may concern: When this is read, I will be dead a year—by my own hand. Last week I was told I might have cancer, and yesterday confirmed the diagnosis with a specialist. Inoperable. Since I do not wish to be reduced to ridicule by pain and fear, I am ending it now, arranging it so that one of my so-called friends will be convicted of my murder. A conviction each of them more richly deserves than I do this death sentence passed upon me by nature.'

"That's a matter of opinion," said Hoffe.

There was the snap of a cigarette lighter. Stalker's note started to burn. Each person already had his own videotape.

Damn! I should have foreseen that none of them would honor the last wishes of a poor, dying, betrayed man.

It was one of the Victorian novelists, I believe, who said that when you go into an attorney's office, you will have to pay for it, first or last.

What I have realized only too late, alas, is that this holds true even if you're the attorney.

Dori and I took a splendid weekend at a San Francisco hotel to celebrate our wedding anniversary. Shortly thereafter, Matt Bruccoli asked me to write a story for his new magazine, A Matter of Crime. *I had just read a newspaper article about a little-known sleep disorder called apnea, and remembered what we had used to keep the champagne cold for our anniversary. I combined both elements in a sort of goofy tale about an ex-pro football player turned private eye faced with a unique murder technique.*

SMART GUYS DON'T SNORE

I was calf-deep in the ivy outside Eric Goldthorpe's bedroom window, listening to him snore like a semi-load of scrap iron going over the Grapevine into L.A. When I'd arrived seven minutes earlier, a tall, skinny guy in a loud sports coat too big for him and a hat too small, wearing shades at 11:48 p.m., was just letting himself out the front door.

He moved easy but looked husky enough to take candy from a baby only if the baby hadn't started teething yet. After the phone message I'd gotten, however, I'd had to check that Goldthorpe was okay inside his converted one-story carriage house. Hence, Krajewski among the nightingales.

The snorer creaked the bedsprings rolling over, then started again. I backed away before the vibrations brought down the slate shingles. Hell, I wasn't even really hired yet.

Back on the nighttime San Francisco street in my Toyota, I opened my thermos of tea and listened to the crickets and tree frogs. No mosquitoes; Pacific Heights was out of their price range. Down the block where the skinny guy had gone, an auto started, then a black Lincoln limo with personalized plates whispered by, a blonde with long, shimmering hair driving.

I ran a mental checklist. Goldthorpe was inside, snoring safely away. I had the front covered, and I'd hear anyone trying to come over the chain-link fence at the back. Eight in the morning, as suggested in his phone message, would be time enough to find out who was trying to kill my soon-to-be client, and why.

But at 3:29 a.m., a prowlie from a cruising black-and-white pointed his Police Positive at me through the window. I stepped out, hands in plain sight, and assumed the position. Pacific Heights isn't Beverly Hills, but even so, all that growth capital makes cops tense.

After patting me down, they told me the sort of thing cops tell a six-foot-seven, 289-pound man they catch with a gun in Pacific Heights at three in the morning. I told them the sort of thing I always tell cops. None of them has ever actually tried to do it, but I keep suggesting and hoping.

An insomniac neighbor had "happened" to see me—hanging off the drainpipe by her fingernails, perhaps?—and had phoned the police. We finally went to wake Goldthorpe so he could confirm he'd called me. We found the front door unlocked and Goldthorpe in bed where I'd heard him snoring three hours before.

Except that now he was dead.

Homicide Inspector Red Delaney, a lanky, sad-eyed guy with freckles and carroty hair gone gray, was in the barrel that night. I figured him for an easy lay, since I had only the truth to tell on this one; and besides, he'd remained a die-hard Raider fan even after the switch from the Bay Area.

But then his boss showed up, not quite as wide as a barn door nor ugly as a griffin, but in that league.

Delaney looked surprised. I looked surprised. Damn few homicide chiefs turn out for the routine stiff at dawn.

"I'm Captain Pritchard," he snapped.

I batted my eyes at him. "Peekaboo," I said.

He turned to Delaney. "Who is this clown?"

"Thaddeus Krajewski. They called him 'Bonecrack' when he was with the Raiders because—"

"I've heard all about you, Krajewski. Big mouth, bitty brain. I'm not taking any crap off you, understand?"

"Does that mean I'm under arrest?" I trilled. To Delaney, I explained, "He likes to say 'Peekaboo' at the perps before he claps the nippers on 'em."

Actually, "Peekaboo" came from his days on the dicky-jerk patrol, busting flamers in downtown men's rooms: Straights coming in for a whiz were outraged at being offered three minutes of true love by a guy with dusty knees. Word was that in those days if you were prominent, married, with a lot to lose, Peekaboo might mislay the tape of your transgression—for a kill fee.

"Okay, Krajewski, by the numbers," he said in a tired voice. "Just for drill. No conjecture."

An electronic flash splattered white light around the bedroom. A man with no more chin than Barry Manilow was lifting prints off the bedside table onto clear plastic rectangles. I yawned abruptly; it had been a long night, getting longer, but I was suddenly wide awake, impatient to get back to my office.

"I came off a case last night at ten-thirty, checked the answering machine at my office and—"

"What case?"

I shook my head. "I might tell a grand jury. Not you." He

was silent. "An Eric Goldthorpe had left a message that his life was in danger and maybe he wanted to hire me. He told me to come around to his house at 8:00 a.m. He didn't say whether he was looking for a bodyguard or an investigator, so—"

"I want that tape!"

I just nodded. "Since he said his life was in danger, I thought I'd maybe not wait for morning. The lights were out, but this other man came out of the house." I described him. "I heard Goldthorpe still snoring, so—"

"Why couldn't the skinny guy have been him?" asked Delaney.

"Goldthorpe's trust fund was something like the gross national product of Canada," I said. "Poor bastard had to do the society whirl on just the interest and the coffee-import company he also inherited. Such men may not be dangerous, but they get their picture in the papers a lot. He would have outweighed the skinny guy by a hundred pounds."

The phone rang. It was the M.E. with a preliminary on cause of death. Red Delaney listened, taking notes, nodding every now and then and grunting. Finally he said, "Thanks, Oscar," and hung up. He grinned at me.

"Saved from the chair, Bonecrack. Natural causes. Looks like Goldthorpe died of apnea."

I screwed up my face in obvious puzzlement. "Apnea?"

"Respiratory problem in some overweight men. Their throat closes down as they sleep, so they quit breathing for periods ranging from a few seconds to a couple of minutes. Can happen a couple of hundred times a night."

Goldthorpe had quit snoring for quite a while before he rolled over and started again. I said so. Red shrugged.

"See? Sometimes they just don't start again, period."

Peekaboo said suddenly, "I've heard that snorers get dumber as they get older—brain damage from oxygen starvation. Anything in that, Krajewski?"

"I don't know, I don't snore," I said with great dignity.

He jerked a thumb at the door. "Come in tomorrow to make a formal statement—and bring that phone-machine tape with you."

At my office in Coppola's flatiron building, I ran a copy of the Goldthorpe message. He had a chewy, indistinct voice, as if he were eating caramels, but his words were clear enough.

"Eric Goldthorpe, 2544 Jackson Street. I might need a private cop and somebody gave me your name. Ah . . . somebody's maybe trying to kill me, so just for drill, maybe I want to hire you. Here. Eight o'clock tomorrow morning."

I put the copy into the phone machine, the original that Peekaboo wanted for the police file in a desk drawer, and lay down on my seven-foot office couch to think about it. Why, if the death was by natural causes, was the skinny guy wearing a coat that was too big and a hat that was too small?

On the other hand, what the hell business was it of mine? My client was dead before I was hired. If at least two different people were playing games, was an ex-Raider lineman smart enough to figure out who and why? Wasn't he maybe just smart enough to stay out of it?

I wrestled with such cosmic questions for fifteen seconds and then fell asleep. Actor Victor Mature'd had the couch custom-made in the '40s because he was so big and liked to lie down a lot; I'd bought it secondhand in the '80s for the same reasons.

"You sure snore loud. I thought the elevator was breaking down while I was on my way up here."

The blonde had her back to the curved bow window with WE NEVER SLEEP backward on the glass. WE NEVER SLEEP had been a good joke when I'd opened the office three years before, to avoid becoming the local TV sportscaster that ex-football players are supposed to be when they grow up. Now its rich humor had paled; who likes to get caught snoring on the office couch?

"The door was open. Honest." She had a little-girl voice in a big-girl body, like sexy little fingers on your spine. When I didn't say anything, she added, "Anyway, I read in the *Chronicle* that people who snore aren't as smart as people who don't."

That joke was getting a little old too. I grunted and sat up on the edge of the couch to look her over frankly. It bothered her as much as a swimmer bothers a shark. Long and lithe. Gleaming hair almost to the small of her back. Skirt slit all the way to whoops, as they say in the columns, showing a lot of leg. Sheena of the Jungle, Penthouse Pet of the Year.

"I snore and I played pro football for eleven years," I told her. "That sort of argues your case, doesn't it?"

At the sink in the corner I splashed water on my face, whuffling and blowing like a grampus. When I turned back, she was stalking me like a cat, hand in her purse. Watching her gliding tread clicked something inside my head. On TV she would have taken out a nickel-plated .22 and shot me in the duodenal ulcer I wasn't going to live long enough to de-velop. In real life, she took out a roll of hundreds heavy enough to drive a tent peg.

"My name is Judi Anderson-Powell. I want to hire you."

"My lucky day. One client dies in the night, another shows up in the morning. *Très* convenient." I gave her my sexy grin, the one compounded of equal parts of lust and greed that somehow seems to never get me a score. "As Mr. Kerouac was fond of saying, Wow, gee whiz, and whew!"

She giggled. "You talk funny."

"You ought to hear me when I'm awake."

But fun time was over. Her eyes got very round and serious. "I *always* forget to pay bills and things, and now the bank has repossessed my husband's company car. He'll just *kill* me if he finds out it was taken." She wiggled her assets around. "It's worth a thousand dollars if you get it back for me."

Every private eye ever born is bright enough to take a thousand bucks for a couple of hours' work. I got the details from her, the money to bail out the car, and my thousand— all in cash. Plus the Marin address where I was supposed to deliver the car. She'd run me back to town.

Alone, I had a quick shower and shave and rechecked the phone machine copy of Goldthorpe's call. Yeah. It figured. *Somebody* wasn't letting me drop this case. I ran the address she had given me through the Marin County crisscross directory that lists by addresses as well as names, then called SRS in Sacramento, which runs licenses, autos, and individuals through the DMV, to ask for a check of Eric Goldthorpe; there had been no car parked by the carriage house. Finally, I called the Stanford Sleep Center for a chat about apnea.

I considered my findings with a buffalo sandwich and a Pauli Girl at Tommy's Joynt, a garish, red short-order emporium that has been on the corner of Van Ness and Geary since 1922 and has some of the best food, beers, and characters in town. My first pro-bowl year, a couple of hotshot publishers from back East had bought me lunch there while trying to convince me I should write a book about pro football. When I decided to retire, they decided to shelve the book. I didn't object. As Ovid said, *Leve fit quad bene fertur onus:* Get screwed cheerfully.

I went through the Hall of Justice detectors at the Bryant Street entrance of the cold, gray concrete shoebox and up to homicide to dictate my statement. Peekaboo came in as I was finishing. He'd decided I was human after all; he said he'd just come from watching Goldthorpe get sliced up.

"The autopsy turn up anything?"

He gave a grunt of what could have been derision. "Exotic poisons? Rare drugs? The bite of a deadly South African mamba?"

"I'd settle for the utterly ordinary: the curare-tipped nib of a goose-quill pen thrust between the second and third ribs and into the heart."

"No contusions, no punctures. No results yet on drugs and poisons, but everything is consistent with death by apnea. Where's that tape I asked for?"

"I forgot to bring it."

"Forgot? Or erased it by mistake?"

I looked sheepish. "You know how it is, Captain."

"You screwed up and erased it! Well, what the hell did I expect, ten years of three-hundred-pound guys sitting on your head?" Then he shrugged. "Oh, hell, when the coroner's report comes in we'll close the file anyway—death by natural causes."

"Then I'll be on my merry way," I said "I've got a nice dirty buck to make."

"Dirtier than most," Peekaboo allowed judiciously.

The repo outfit was at 340 11th Street, a midblock, two-story brick building that had been a laundry when I'd been playing left tackle for Lowell. This was a commercial district turning lavender, with a gay bar on the corner and a bathhouse down the street that was probably hurting for trade since AIDS.

A couple of agency field men were making out a condition report on a new T-bird run up across the sidewalk, its nose poked in between the heavy, slid-open doors of their storage garage. When I came up they stopped working with identical wary stances.

"Nice car," I said.

The shorter one unobtrusively picked up a tire iron from the open trunk and gave me the sort of grin you see on the skulls in anatomy labs. "Yours?" He was plum-black, very wide in the shoulders and narrow in the hips. Always beware of well-conditioned men whose necks are as wide as their heads.

"You don't know?"

"We didn't stop to chat with the registered owner when we grabbed it."

"Not mine."

He relaxed fractionally. The tall one said, "We thought maybe you'd come to tuck it under your arm and take it home."

He was white, about six feet, rangy, almost too pretty at first glance for the business; but the cold blue eyes above his hawk nose said he was able to carry the weight. He was Ballard, the other one was Heslip. I said I was Thaddeus Krajewski.

"Hot damn, Bonecrack Krajewski," said Heslip. "Nose tackle for the Raiders. Before that, All-American at Notre Dame."

Ballard said, "Forty-niner games, you spent so much time on top of Montana I thought you guys would get married."

"Fickle bastard gave back my ring when I retired." I recognized Heslip then. "You used to headline fight cards at the Cow Palace."

"I was gonna be middleweight champ of the world, but I quit the game when I had to start banging my head against the wall in the morning to get my brain started."

The car was a black Lincoln limo with only 11,000 on the clock, smoked rear windows, and a personalized license plate, IMPORT. I caught up the bank's payments and all charges, which weren't too heavy. It had been a voluntary turn-in; they'd found it parked outside that morning with the keys through the mail slot. They gave me a champagne case full of personal possessions that had been in the car, which I stuck in the tire well. I took off, leaving my Toyota in their fenced parking area overnight.

The Lincoln was quite a boat, with a mobile phone I used to call Sacramento to get my rundown from SRS on Goldthorpe's car. Yeah. As I'd thought. Waiting in rush-hour traffic on the Golden Gate Bridge approach, I tried to figure out if the personal effects had any hidden or extended meaning: A box of Kleenex, seven packets of rock-hard bubble gum, three three-pound cans of coffee, a flashlight, a *Nurse Romance* comic book, a charge card receipt for a case of Dom Perignon and ten pounds of dry ice, and two spent .44 Magnum shell casings.

Not immediately illuminating, not unless you posited an allergic bubble-blower who broke a tooth on the over-age gum, tried to keep his mind off the discomfort with a *Nurse* comic book and ice-cold champagne when he couldn't get the coffee open, finally despaired and shot himself with a .44 Magnum.

Conjecture, like statistics, can be vastly overrated.

I crawled across the bridge into Marin with the rest of the rush-hour ants. Forget about peacock feathers and yuppies and hot tubs and dope dealers who weigh their money by the pound: It still doesn't get any better than Marin County. Civic Center has sold out to the builders, but for a few more years you'll still be able to find open country, sweeping vistas, and an individual life-style not dependent on the national whim. Southern Marin can go the distance with Beverly Hills any day; outlying areas still have not only some hippie enclaves, but even a few shaggy unregenerate beats whose jeans haven't seen soap since 1955.

It was dark by the time the winding blacktop off Route 1 took me up Mt. Tamalpais toward the address the blonde had given me, in one of the little residential pockets above Mill Valley. I could smell the dusty pollen of the Scotch broom that was taking over the mountain. When the other car came up too fast in my rearview, about a half-mile short of Judi's turnoff, I hit the window button just in time.

Something stubby that looked like an Israeli Uzi poked out of their open window. Muzzle flashes illuminated their intent, brown murderous faces. Would-be murderous; the slugs sparked and whined harmlessly against the Lincoln's Kevlar plating, ricocheting off the armored glass windows.

Fuck them. I was in three tons of steel. I jerked the wheel over, hard. There was the shriek of metal on metal, and the sedan soared up and out, already turning in midair as it went over the rim of the road and out of sight. I could picture it, crashing sideways down through the stand of trees in a burst of shiny eucalyptus leaves like an injured koi swimming on its side through a cloud of silver scales. I didn't bother to stop. Anyone tough enough to walk away from that one was tough enough to find his own way home.

Man, they were not near my conscience; they made love to that employment.

The house clung to the hillside by concrete fingernails above a sheer fall of greasewood, sage, and broom. There was a sporty new Mustang ragtop in the carport on the roof; the bedrooms were in the basement, and the view out the living room picture-windows was a stunning one-eighty of the distant city and sprawling bay, black-and-white in color.

Judi seemed genuinely glad to see me; she gave me a big hug when I came through the door, then stepped back with a puzzled look on her face. "You're trembling. Are you all right?"

Three men are dead. Are you all right?

"Nothing that a glass of champagne wouldn't fix."

She clapped her hands in delight. "I have some Dom Perignon on ice because . . ."

She let that drift away as if it led into an abrupt mental cul-de-sac she didn't want to enter. While she went to the wet bar in the corner, I admired the view. Her see-through point d'esprit lace chemise showed that she had a great deal to see, and her short red silk robe, edged in black lace and left carelessly open, did very little to obscure the sights.

"Expecting your husband?" I asked in a husky voice. The deaths of the three killers and my concomitant survival had left me as tumescent as a snort of ground rhino horn. In the midst of death we are in life.

"He was due home this evening but . . ." she shrugged as she set a bottle of Dom Perignon on the countertop. "But he's away."

"Far away?" I was feeling a little hoarse.

"Overnight away."

I cleared my throat. "You said he would kill you if he knew you'd let his car get repossessed." I paused dramatically. "I just killed three guys getting it back for you." She started to give me that little-girl giggle, then stopped at what she saw in my eyes. I gestured. "Go look at your car."

I stood at the picture window pretending to look at the view. In the heat of pro-football combat you say, even do, a lot of destructive things. But most of that is deliberate intimidation, or a tactical ploy to get the other guy mad so he'll foul you in front of the ref and draw a penalty.

This was three men *dead.* Yeah, they'd planned to kill me, and hadn't succeeded only because the Lincoln was armorplated and because professional athletes are trained to act first and think afterward. But just maybe they were nearer my conscience than I'd thought in my first flush of continued existence.

Judi's hands were on my arms, turning me from the window. Her hungry face was against mine, her little-girl's voice was saying, "Poor darling! Don't think about it . . ."

The silk robe was just a crimson flame on the rug at our feet; the black lace dissolved between my fingers like spider webs. Her flesh was feverish to the touch. For a little while there was no thought, no conscience, nothing but thrust against yielding thrust, raking nails, and finally her soft cries of completion to bring me to my own.

Afterward we sat on the couch drinking icy Dom Perignon and looking at the view. I told her about the attack. She shook her head in the semidarkness, her pale hair shimmering with the movement like ripe cornsilk. It had smelled of herbal shampoo when my face had been buried in it.

"But who would want to follow you and . . . try to kill you?"

"Probably somebody who thought I was your husband. What does he do that he has to drive around in an armorplated car?"

"He's a gemstone importer. He's in Europe right now. . . ."

"Yeah. Somebody thought he was just coming back from Antwerp or Rotterdam with a pocketful of uncut diamonds."

As if chilled by the realization that she was a married woman who had just broken her vows on the floor of her living room with a man she had met that morning, she got up and started pacing the room with fluid, gliding grace.

"When I looked at the car," she said as she moved, "I didn't see . . . oh, I had some groceries and—"

"Those damned repossessors!" I exclaimed. "I'll go back and get the personal possessions from them tonight."

"No! Please!" Then the urgency departed her voice. "Don't bother. All of it can be easily replaced."

I told her I'd better take the Lincoln when I went to report the attack. She agreed. There was an awkward moment when we parted; we were suddenly back to what we really were, two strangers who had met, connected, now were shearing off again. What we'd needed from each other we'd gotten.

At Tam Junction I wiped all the places I had touched inside the bullet-pocked limo, retrieved the personal property from the trunk, and left the car in the parking lot under the freeway. I also called the cops, leaving no name, to say it had been involved in the shoot-out in the foothills. They'd have a lot of fun tying the bullet-acned Lincoln in with the three dead men, especially when the registration checked back to another dead man.

After the bus ride into the city, I couldn't sleep. It felt like the night before the Super Bowl. I got up and heated a cup of Red Rose tea in the microwave, turned on MTV, and tried to analyze what was bothering me.

Yeah! The receipt for the champagne and the dry ice. It came back from some forgotten chem course. Dry ice! Plain old carbon dioxide. An odorless, colorless, incombustible gas. Found in natural springs or processed from coal or natural gas through carbohydrate fermentation. Some .03 percent of the atmosphere at sea level. Produced in the human body at varying rates during exertion by the burning of blood sugar, then liberated from the venous blood into the lungs and exhaled. Used in carbonated soft drinks and in fire extinguishers and, when called dry ice, to keep things cold.

Finally I could sleep.

When I retired from football I dropped 22 pounds from my playing weight of 311, and I work hard to keep it off. I have a slantboard and a rack of dumbbells at the apartment for quick workouts when I'm on a case. I did a concentrated forty-five minutes and after my shower called a cab, then Red Delaney at the Hall of Justice. By luck he was in.

"I know Goldthorpe is supposed to have died of natural causes," I said, "but indulge me. In the postmortem lab work were there any traces of—"

"What do you mean, supposed? *Did* die of natural causes."

"Fine. Were sedative traces found in his blood workup?"

I heard pages turning. "Yeah. Probably ten milligrams of something like Dalmane. But with an alcohol level of only point zero-zero-one, definitely not enough to affect cause of death, if that's what you're thinking. "

"I'm not thinking anything."

"Your usual state."

"Just a little old headpiece filled with straw. Come to think of it, that's the trouble with this whole damned scenario—too many people think that smart guys don't snore."

My cab honked down in the street. I hung up and went out. I found Heslip and Ballard in one of the back rooms at the repo agency, knee-deep in an incredible jumble of possessions—old clothes and flashlights and tool kits and letters and payment books and road maps and magazines and boxes of condoms and, by contrast, an unopened package of Pampers as big as a trash bucket.

"A burglary of the personal-property storage lockers, can you *believe* that?" demanded Ballard glumly.

I had expected it, the final figure in my equation. I now was sure of *who* and *how*—I just didn't know *why*. Yet.

"What'd they get?"

"Who can tell?" said Heslip. "The personal possessions in a repo don't generally make me want to grab them and take off for a country with no extradition."

When I got to Goldthorpe's coffee-import offices and warehouse in China Basin off Third Street, there was the Mustang convertible. Of course: the old asp-in-the-bosom scenario. I played Twenty Questions with a couple of yardmen who had gotten the idea I was a cop. No, Goldthorpe's death hadn't really interrupted much. Coffee prices being what they were, the business was going down the toilet anyway. He'd spent most of his time in South America, buying coffee. Better talk to Judi Anderson.

I kicked a tire of the Mustang convertible. "This hers?"

"Yeah." The young one had a dusting of acne across his chin and a dirty laugh. "Not that she paid for it herself."

"Shut up, Harry," said the older one, much too belatedly.

I left them glaring at one another and crossed the warehouse with its burlap bags wearing bonded warehouse seals and a heavy aroma of roasted coffee beans. A hallway went past the rest rooms to the front offices. Here functional gave way to front: hardwood walls, original oils, heavy-legged furniture to suggest an old-line firm. I kept poking my head into doorways and saying "Pardon me" until I found her alone behind a fancy hardwood desk.

The shimmering blond hair was tucked up into a sort of bun at the back of her head, giving her an old-fashioned look, and her perfect features were either without makeup or with makeup so artful that it looked like none. She had a lot of different looks. Her eyes popped wide when she saw me. She flowed out of her chair and across the room toward me.

"Thaddeus! What . . ."

I gave her my biggest, dumbest grin. "Hey, it's okay that you lied to me about being somebody's wife when really you were Goldthorpe's girlfriend. What else could you do, right?"

She looked around nervously. "Oh, Thaddeus, we can't talk here, but I desperately want . . ." Inspiration flooded her face. "My place again? Tonight? Then I can explain everything."

I said that was swell. She put her hands on my upper arms, as she had when she'd turned me away from the window the night before. Her face was ashamed.

"I . . . didn't know what else to do. I . . . I had to get the car back, and I was afraid that maybe those men . . ."

"Hey, sweetie, I said it was okay."

"I'm so scared and I just . . . I want someone to tell me what to do so I'll be safe. . . ."

"Sure." I almost licked my lips. "Like last night."

She cast another quick look up and down the hall, then went up on tiptoe to kiss me. It wasn't a peck. "Yes!" she breathed into my mouth, then added fiercely, "Like last night!"

Heading home, the afternoon *Examiner*'s headlines about the dead guys in Marin and Goldthorpe's bullet-pocked Lincoln stopped me. They had been Colombian nationals. Colombia is where the coffee comes from, and Goldthorpe had been a coffee importer. Obviously, a hit over whose coffee was the richest kind.

Like hell.

Watch a man minutely examining something unknown and—creationists be damned—you will see a risen ape, not a fallen angel. We are suddenly chimpanzees turning over rocks for the grubs beneath. I call it the Chimp Trip. I got the champagne case from where I'd stashed it and laid everything out on my kitchen table. The flashlight was a most promising place to hide something, but it proved a bust. The coffee made a mountain on newspapers spread across the table, but without treasure inside.

Would I know what I was looking for even if I found it? Something worth paying me a thousand bucks to recover. Something worth three brown-faced men, dealt out of the action, waiting in ambush for whoever might show up in the dead Goldthorpe's car.

Then I got smart. If it was conceivable that someone could secrete something inside a can of coffee and reseal it afterward, how much easier with a packet of stale bubble gum? It was anticlimactic, it was so mundane.

In one package, the Giants baseball card wasn't a baseball card. It was a claim check.

The bus station on Seventh off Market was its usual self: big, noisy, echoing, barren, cold, filled with people whose best years were behind them or, in a few cases, yet to come. Minorities, the elderly, servicemen, the unemployed and the unemployable, the third-generation welfare recipients. And of course the rapists and muggers and pimps, sliding through the crowds seeking warm meat to feed their varied psychoses.

The woman behind the counter handed me a large gym bag, the sort that will hold your sweats and Reeboks and two pair of sweat socks and a towel and a jump rope and your Heavy Hands grippers. Whatever this one held still smelled of coffee. And I remembered a feature of coffee: A beagle would go baying right by a rabbit that hid in a bin of the stuff.

I opened it down on Townsend Street, where I had unused railroad tracks on one side, empty warehouses on the other, and could pour sweat unobserved. I thought I knew what was in the bag, but there were, after all, four people dead. Better not add half a city block of shoppers. But what was inside was like that verse in Isaiah: The valleys were exalted, the hills were made low, the crooked straight, and the rough places plain.

I knew it all, then, except how he had met her. I didn't have to wonder how she had gotten him to go along with her: She could have gotten an archbishop to rifle the poor box.

Peekaboo wasn't available, but I found Red Delaney in the low-ceilinged, gloomy cafeteria under the Hall of Justice. He swore a lot but in the end got me her rap sheet. Not much, but enough: material witness in a murder case three years before. Never charged with anything. We talked seriously then. I seemed to keep doing things to Red's coloring; his face had become as gray as his hair had by the time I left him.

Then I talked to Peekaboo. He was, after all, captain of homicide. I made a few remarks to loosen him up and, poor sport he, got back a visual *mano nera* from his cold fish-eyes.

"One of these days, Krajewski, I'm going to have you in an alley all alone. And then, just for drill—"

"Just for drill, you're gonna bruise my knuckles with your nose. I know. But first, I'm going to make you look silly at the same time that I give you a big, juicy Murder One bust. . . ."

Judi threw open the door dramatically and kissed me on the mouth, breathless, eyes sparkling, bringing the warmth and smell of a hardwood fire with her. She backed into the living room, leading me with my paws in her hands. The lights were out; the fire cast moving patterns of light and shadow across the floor and walls; and the slow-seething vapor settled around a big ice bucket on the white fake-bearskin rug.

"What have you got in there? Rocket fuel?"

"Something more potent. Dom Perignon."

"What're we celebrating?"

She let go of my hands and whirled around in the middle of the floor, the long tails of her white silk tailored blouse billowing out like a miniskirt. She fell against me giddily.

"Being rich. Being free." Her eyes, suddenly enormous, sought mine. In her little-girl voice she added, as a question, "Being safe?" Then with urgency, "if you'll be loyal to me, Thaddeus, then I know I'll be safe."

"Hey, was Sam loyal to Brigid? You can count on me, kid." She snuggled into my arms again. I tried to keep my head when all about me were losing theirs. I said, "Your burglar at the repo agency last night didn't find the personal possessions out of Goldthorpe's armored limo because I took them with me."

She smiled up into my face lazily. "What did *you* find?"

"A claim check." I stepped back to take a square of cardboard out of my jacket pocket. "I haven't had a chance to pick up whatever Goldthorpe checked on it, but . . ." I paused. "But I think we've just become partners."

She didn't speak. She kissed me.

"Then that's settled," I said with a big, dumb grin. "Let's go find out if it's what I think it is."

"First, champagne!" she exclaimed.

The Dom Perignon had two long-stemmed champagne glasses stuck down into the dry ice beside it. General Sternwood had said champagne should be drunk cold as Valley Forge, and this was. Time—and bottles—passed for us, side by side on that silly rug. Dom Perignon I don't get every day. Sometimes I poured, sometimes she poured. It started to get stuffy in there. The firelight played mysteries across her flawless features.

"What do you think we'll find, Thaddeus?"

"A lot of uncut cocaine," I said drowsily.

Her eyes got very big. "Cocaine! You mean Eric was—"

"Now, sweetie," I chided thickly, "we gotta be hones' to each other. It was you got him to do it, after the interest of daddy's trust fund wasn't enough anymore. . . ." She was silent for a long moment, then found a smile. It was small and tentative, like a kitten coming out from under a strange bed. "It was easy, you had a Colombian connection. I 'membered your picture from the newspaper. . . ." So I was lying, so I'd seen it in her rap sheet. "Some drug murders . . ."

"You're a rather clever man, darling."

"He could bring it in easily—the smell of coffee throws off the drug dogs at customs. The real danger would be in the transfer of the coke to the distributors. The Colombians."

I peered at her again in the candlelight. The smile had gotten more sure of itself, like the same kitten a day later.

She said, "The repo idea was my contribution."

I nodded. "It's cute and devious." I had a distinct impression I was slurring my words. "He stashes the drugs at the bus depot left-luggage. After he's been paid, he leaves the claim check in a pack of bubble gum in his car, which he makes sure is repossessed. The Colombians redeem it, get the claim check and the coke. Anything goes wrong, he's not tied into it."

"I think it was a very good plan," she said a little defensively. I laughed heartily and held out my glass.

"Sure, f'r you."

She poured. I spilled most of mine on the rug. I laid down on my back, the glass balanced on my chest. She smiled.

"Not for Eric?"

"Ol' Eric, he dies right on time, you get the money he's already collected. Then you offer a guy 'way too much money to redeem the car before the Colombians do. You get both the dope *an'* the money. . . ." She was an indistinct black cutout against the flickering firelight. I was definitely stumbling over words. "Didn't 'spect me being outside that night, hadda leave wearin' Eric's sports jacket and hat. Jacket too big, hat too small—'cause of all that hair coiled up underneath it."

She said softly, "Eric died from apnea."

But I was on a roll. "I saw you drive by in his limo *without* your shades an' hat. Persh . . . personalized plate: IMPORT. Same car I 'deemed th' next day." I yawned suddenly. "Whassa difference, an'way? We go get the coke, we're rich. . . ."

My head dropped back on the rug. All of a sudden I was

snoring. After about a minute, she said, softly, "Thaddeus? Honey?" I grunted and rolled around and didn't breathe for twenty seconds. Then I started to snore again. She'd doctored my champagne with Dalmane, but it was easy to fight: I had a lot of muscle tissue to absorb it.

I felt her hand slide into my pocket for the claim check.

"Goodbye, fool," she said softly.

Even with my eyes shut, I could follow the sounds of her quick movements. Taking her glass out to the kitchen to wash it. Sloshing water into the bucket as if ice had melted there, leaving it near me on the rug, along with the empty champagne bottles. Setting the big clump of dry ice beside my head.

Dry ice. Pure carbon dioxide. Colorless, tasteless, odorless. A heavy gas, displacing the air as it melts, settling as a layer around Goldthorpe's head, around my head. You're asleep, lightly sedated. You breathe carbon dioxide instead of oxygen. At 3 percent, 100 times normal, respiration doubles. At 6 percent, you're panting. If you're awake, you're confused. At 10 percent, you thrash and gasp, but it's too late for you.

Because at 30 percent, you're dead.

Meanwhile, the dry ice would melt away, the free gas dissipate. Everything gone. Carbon dioxide, unlike water, does not leave a wet spot. Tests of the blood from your corpse show only high concentrations of carbon dioxide—as death by apnea does.

Case closed.

The front door closed quietly. I already was breathing heavier than normal from the gas. "Not such a fool," I said aloud. The net would close around her any moment.

A gun went off outside!

I jumped to my feet, ran out and up to the carport,

stopped to stare at Judi, crumpled beside her open Mustang door. I went down on one knee beside her. No pulse. I looked up at Peekaboo.

"You shot her," I said stupidly. "You weren't supposed to shoot her."

He still had his service revolver in his hand, a shocked expression on his face. "I . . . I told her to stop. She went for something in her purse, I thought . . . it was a gun. . . ."

I stood up slowly. She'd murdered one man, put me in a position where I killed three more; she'd planned to kill me. . . . I didn't know what I felt, except self-disgust. Some smart guy! I should have seen it coming.

"Probably a claim check," I said dully.

"Yeah. I know that now." He held it up. "Evidence."

I shook my head. "The trouble is, Peekaboo, people really do think big guys are dumb." I felt the anger grow in me. I let it. I liked it. "We hulk around; we have fingers like sausages; our voices are too deep and our chins too blue. Fat guys can't be tragic; big guys can't be smart."

I took a step toward him.

"But ever since I was a kid, bigger than anybody in my class, I had to be smarter, too. *Had* to be. How come the cops rousted me outside Goldthorpe's house? I'd parked where nobody could see into my car. So the report that brought them was a phony. Why? When we found him dead, I knew it was because I'd been supposed to show up the next morning and find the body."

Peekaboo's big, harsh face was puzzled.

"You're telling me Goldthorpe *didn't* call you?"

I gestured at Judi's dead, deflated body. The anger, blunted by talk, spurted again. "Of course not. She and her partner needed him dead—but found quickly so his death by natural causes would be established and the case closed.

No matter what some P.I. without any proof might say about threats."

He shook his head, amused, perhaps, if we hadn't been standing over the corpse of a woman he just had killed.

"I gotta give you that she's a killer—though I thought you were nuts earlier when you said so. But a partner? C'mon."

I nodded. "You, Peekaboo."

"*Me?* I never even met—"

"Interrogated her two years ago in connection with the drug bust of a Colombian—I killed him on this mountain last night. It's in her rap sheet, Peekaboo, but I didn't need that to know it was your disguised voice on my phone tape. First you show up at Goldthorpe's, not even on duty, and then—"

"You're nuts, Krajewski!"

"And then, just for drill, Judi comes and erases the tape in my phone machine the next morning before she wakes me up. That afternoon you didn't give a damn if I gave you the tape or not—because she'd already told you she'd erased it."

His eyes had gotten bleak. "Did you say, 'Just for drill'?"

"Yeah. Not a common locution. You say it, too often. The voice on the tape said it too."

He chuckled nastily. "Well, without the tape to run voice-print comparisons off of . . ."

To show how smart I really am, I kept talking. "Oh, I've got that. Judi just erased a copy I left in the machine—"

He shot me.

The slug took me high on the chest near the collarbone, nonlethal, because I already was moving even though my conscious mind didn't know he was going to shoot. It felt about like a blocker's elbow when you're rushing the passer, but, always articulate, I said something like "Arghhhh!"

He got off two more shots, both wild because my big paw already was pulping his hand around the revolver. He screamed, then I had him bent backward over the hood, choking him, not caring which shattered first, his neck vertebrae or his spinal cord. I was liking this work; I was liking it fine. Just like they always say, the first killing is the hard one.

But then some fool was yelling and bouncing a gun butt off my skull. "Bonecrack—*no!* He has to stand trial! No!"

I went down. Peekaboo was on his face and knees beside me, making retching noises, his face purple. I tried to kick him in the temple but was too tired. I peered up at Red Delaney. Blood running down my face youthed him, made his hair red again instead of gray. He crouched beside me, revolver still in hand.

"How bad is that shoulder?"

"Like a dumb mouth it doth ope its ruby lips."

He stood up. "Jesus you're an asshole, Bonecrack."

Peekaboo groaned and rolled onto his side and drooled a little blood.

I said hopefully, "Let me finish him so he can't figure out some way to get off."

"If they let him off, I'll do it myself."

And such sudden hot rage suffused his features that I knew it was going to be okay. He meant it. Red Delaney played cop the way I'd played nose tackle. No compromise, no quarter. No pity. The bastard started to laugh.

"Let him shoot you, when you *knew* he was guilty! Hell, he was right about brain damage after all. Smart guys *don't* snore."

I tried to tell him to go screw himself, as I always tell the cops to do, but I was already asleep.

Not snoring, dammit!

I got snuck into an Explosives and Sabotage Devices anti-terrorist course for law enforcement officers at Fort Ord, California, because the instructor was an old friend. I got to blow up a lot of stuff and spend enough hours with an FBI profiler attending the course to learn that terrorists, be they of the left or right, foreign or domestic, are always with us and always the same. So I wrote this tale of an urban terrorist who is clever, cruel, amoral, manipulative, and utterly without pity.

WATCH FOR IT

Eric's first one. The very first.

And it went up early.

If I'd been in my apartment on Durant, with the window open, I probably would have heard it. And probably, at 4:30 in the morning, would have thought like any straight that it had been a truck back-fire. But I'd spent the night balling Elizabeth over in San Francisco while Eric was placing the bomb in Berkeley. With her every minute, I'd made sure, because whatever else you can say about the federal pigs, they're thorough. I'd known that if anything went wrong, they'd be around looking.

Liz and I heard it together on the noon news, when we were having breakfast before her afternoon classes. She teaches freshman English at SF State.

Eric Whitlach, outspoken student radical on the Berkeley campus, was injured early this morning when a bomb he allegedly was placing under a table in the Student Union detonated prematurely. Police said the ex-

103

plosive device was fastened to a clock mechanism set for
9:30, when the area would have been packed with students. The extent of the young activist's injuries is not
known, but—

"God, that's terrible," Liz said with a shudder. She'd
been in a number of upper-level courses with both Eric and
me. "What could have happened to him, Ross, to make him
do . . . something like that?"

"I guess. . . . Well, I haven't seen much of him since
graduation last June . . ." I gestured above the remains of
our eggs and bacon. " 'Student revolutionary'—it's hard to
think of Eric that way." Then I came up with a nice touch.
"Maybe he shouldn't have gone beyond his M.A. Maybe
he should have stopped when we did—before he lost
touch."

When I'd recruited Eric without appearing to, it had
seemed a very heavy idea. I mean, nobody actually expects
this vocal, kinky, Rubin-type radical to go out and set
bombs; because they don't. We usually avoid Eric's sort
ourselves: they have no sense of history, no discipline.
They're as bad as the Communists on the other side of the
street, with their excessive regimentation, their endless
orders from somewhere else.

I stood up. "Well, baby, I'd better get back across the
Bay . . ."

"Ross, aren't you . . . I mean, can't you . . ."

She stopped there, coloring; still a lot of that corrupting
Middle America in her. She was ready to try anything at all
in bed, but to say right out in daylight that she wanted me
to ball her again after class—that still sort of blew her mind.

"I can't, Liz," I said all aw-shucksy, laughing down inside at how *straight* she was. "I *was* his roommate until

four months ago, and the police or somebody might want to ask me questions about him."

I actually thought that they might, and nothing brings out pig paranoia quicker than somebody not available for harassment when they want him. But nobody showed up. I guess they knew that as long as they had Eric they could get whatever they wanted out of him just by shooting electricity into his balls or something, like the French pigs in Algeria. I know how the fascists operate.

Beyond possible questions by the pigs, however, I knew there'd be a strategy session that night in Berkeley. After dark at Zeta Books, on Telegraph south of the campus, is the usual time and place for a meet. Armand Marsh let me in and locked the door behind me; he runs the store for the Student Socialist Alliance as a cover. He's a long skinny redheaded cat with ascetic features and quick nervous mannerisms, and is cell-leader for our three-man focal.

I saw that Danzer was in the mailing room when I got there, as was Benny. I didn't like Danzer being there. Sure, he acted as liaison with other Bay Area locals, but he never went out on operations and so he was an outsider. No outsider can be trusted.

"Benny," said Armand, "how badly is Whitlach really hurt?"

Benny Leland is night administrator for Alta Monte Hospital. With his close-trimmed hair and conservative clothes he looks like the ultimate straight.

"He took a big splinter off the table right through his shoulder. Damned lucky that he had already set it and was on his way out when it blew. Otherwise they'd have just found a few teeth and toes."

"So he'd be able to move around?"

"Oh, sure. The injury caused severe shock, but he's out

of that now; and the wound itself is not critical." He paused to look pointedly at me. "What I don't understand is how the damned thing went off prematurely."

Meaning I was somehow to blame, since I had supplied Eric with the materiel for the bomb. Armand looked over at me too.

"Ross? What sort of device was it?"

"Standard," I said. "Two sticks of dynamite liberated from that P.G. and E. site four months ago. An electric blasting cap with a small battery to detonate it. Alarm dock timer. He was going to carry the whole thing in a gift-wrapped shoe box to make it less conspicuous. There are several ways that detonation could—"

"None of that is pertinent now," interrupted Danzer. His voice was cold and heavy, like his face. He even looked like a younger Raymond Burr. "Our first concern is this: Will the focal be compromised if they break him down and he starts talking?"

"Eric was my best friend before I joined the focal," I said, "and he was my roommate for four years. But once we had determined it was better to use someone still a student than to set this one ourselves, I observed the standard security procedures in recruiting him. He believes the bombing was totally his own idea."

"He isn't even aware of the *existence* of the focal, let alone who's in it," Armand explained. "There's no way that he could hurt us."

Danzer's face was still cold when he looked over at me, but I had realized he *always* looked cold. "Then it seems that Ross is the one to go in after him."

"If there's any need to go at all," said Benny quickly. I knew what he was thinking. Any operation would entail the hospital, which meant he would be involved. He didn't like that. "After all, if he can't hurt us, why not just . . ." He shrugged.

"Just leave him there? Mmmph." Danzer publishes a couple of underground radical newspapers even though he's only twenty-seven, and also uses his presses to run off porn novels for some outfit in L.A. I think he nets some heavy bread. "I believe I can convince you of the desirability of going in after him. If Ross is willing . . ."

"Absolutely." I kept the excitement from my voice. Cold. Controlled. That's the image I like to project. A desperate man, reckless, careless of self. "If anyone else came through that door, Eric would be convinced he was an undercover pig. As soon as he sees me, he'll know that I've come to get him away."

"Why couldn't Ross just walk in off the street as a normal visitor?" asked Danzer.

"There's a twenty-four hour police guard on Whitlach's door." Benny was still fighting the idea of a rescue operation. "Only the doctors and one authorized nurse per shift get in."

"All right. And Ross *must not* be compromised. If he is, the whole attempt would be negated, worse than useless." Which at the moment I didn't understand. "Now let's get down to it."

As Danzer talked, I began to comprehend why he had been chosen to coordinate the activities of the focals. His mind was cold and logical and precise, as was his plan. What bothered me was my role in that plan. But I soon saw the error in my objections. I was Eric's friend, the only one he knew he could trust—and I had brought him into it in the first place. There was danger, of course, but that only made me feel better the more I thought of it. You have to take risks if you are to destroy a corrupt society, because like a snake with a broken back it still has venom on its fangs.

It took three hours to work out the operational scheme.

Alta Monte Hospital is set in the center of a quiet residential area off Ashby Avenue. It used to be easy to approach after dark; just walk to the side entrance across the broad blacktop parking lot. But so many doctors going out to their cars have been mugged by heads looking for narcotics that the lot is patrolled now.

I parked on Benvenue, got the hypo kit and the cherry bombs from the glove box, and slid them into my pocket. The thin strong nylon rope was wound around my waist under my dark blue windbreaker. My breath went up in gray wisps on the chilly wet night air. After I'd locked the car, I held out my hand to look at it by the pale illumination of the nearest street lamp. No tremors. The nerves were cool, man. *I* was cool.

3:23 a.m. by my watch.

In seven minutes, Benny Leland would unlock the small access door on the kitchen loading dock. He would relock it three minutes later, while going back to the staff coffee room from the men's lavatory. I had to get inside during those three minutes or not at all.

3:27

I hunkered down in the thick hedge rimming the lot. My palms were getting sweaty. Everything hinged on a nurse who came off work in midshift because her old man worked screwy hours and she had to be home to babysit her kid. If she was late. . . .

The guard's voice carried clearly on the black misty air. "All finished, Mrs. Adamson?"

"Thank God, Danny. It's been a rough night. We lost

one in post-op that I was sure would make it."

"Too bad. See you tomorrow, Mrs. Adamson."

I had a cherry bomb in my rubber-gloved hand now. I couldn't hear her soft-soled nurse's shoes on the blacktop, but I could see her long thin shadow come bouncing up the side of her car ten yards away. I came erect, threw, stepped back into shadow.

It was beautiful, man; like a sawed-off shotgun in the silent lot. She gave a wonderful scream, full-throated, and the guard yelled. I could hear his heavy feet thudding to her aid as he ran past my section of hedge.

I was sprinting across the blacktop behind his back on silent garage attendant's shoes, hunched as low as possible between the parked cars in case anyone had been brought to a window by the commotion. Without checking my pace, I ran down the kitchen delivery ramp to crouch in the deep shadow under the edge of the loading platform.

Nothing. No pursuit. My breath ragged in my chest, more from excitement than my dash. The watch said 3:31. Beautiful.

I threw a leg up, rolled onto my belly on the platform. Across to the access port in the big overhead accordion steel loading door. It opened easily under my careful fingertips. Benny was being cool, too, producing on schedule for a change. I don't entirely trust Benny.

Hallway deserted, as per the plan. That unmistakable hospital smell. Across the hall, one of those wheeled carts holding empty food trays ready for the morning's breakfasts. Right where it was supposed to be. I put the two cherry bombs on the front left corner of the second tray down, turned, went nine quick paces to the firedoor.

My shoes made slight scuffing noises on the metal runners. By law, hospital firedoors cannot be locked. I checked my watch: in nineteen seconds, Benny Leland would emerge from the men's room and, as he walked back to the staff coffee room, would relock the access door and casually hook the cherry bombs from the tray. I then would have three minutes to be in position.

It had been 150 seconds when I pulled the third-floor firedoor a quarter-inch ajar. No need to risk looking out: I could visualize everything from Benny's briefing earlier.

"Whitlach's room is the last one on the corridor, right next to the fire stairs," he'd said. "I arranged that as part of my administrative duties—actually, of course, in case we *would* want to get to him. The floor desk with the night duty nurse is around an ell and at the far end of the corridor. She's well out of the way. The policeman will be sitting beside Whitlach's door on a metal folding chair. He'll be alone in the hall at that time of night."

Ten seconds. I held out my hand. No discernible tremor.

Benny Leland, riding alone in the elevator from the basement to the fourth floor administrative offices, would just be stopping here at the third floor. As the doors opened, he would punch *four* again; as they started to close, he would hurl his two cherry bombs down the main stairwell, and within seconds would be off the elevator and into his office on the floor above. The pig could only think it had been someone on the stairs.

Whoomp! Whump!

Fantastic, man! Muffled, so the duty nurse far down the corridor and around a corner wouldn't even hear them; but loud enough so the pig, mildly alert for a possible attempt to free Whitlach, would have to check. . . .

I counted ten, pulled open the firedoor, went the six paces to Eric's now unguarded door. Thirty feet away, the pig's beefy blue-clad back was just going through the access doors to the elevator shaft and the main stairwell.

A moment of absolute panic when Eric's door stuck. Then it pulled free and I was inside. Sweat on my hands under the thin rubber gloves. Cool it now, baby.

I could see the pale blur of Eric's face as he started up from his medicated doze. His little night light cast harsh, antiseptic shadows across his lean face. Narrow stubborn jaw, very bright blue eyes, short nose, wiry, tight-curled brown hair. I felt a tug of compassion: he was very pale and drawn.

But then a broad grin lit up his features. *"Ross!"* he whispered. "How in the hell—"

"No time, baby." My own voice was low, too. I already had the syringe out, was stabbing it into the rubber top of the little phial. "The pig will be back from checking out my diversion in just a minute. We have to be ready for him. Can you move?"

"Sure. What do you want me to—"

"Gimme your arm, baby." I jammed the needle into his flesh, depressed the plunger as I talked. "Pain-killer. In case we bump that shoulder getting you out of here, you won't feel anything."

Eric squeezed my arm with his left hand; there were tears in his eyes. How scared that poor cat must have been when he woke up in the hands of the fascist pigs!

"Christ, Ross, I can't believe . . ." He shook his head. "Oh, Jesus right out from under their snouts! You're beautiful, man!"

I got an arm around his shoulders, as the little clock in my mind ticked off the seconds, weighing, measuring the pig's native stupidity against his duty at the door. They have that sense of duty, all right, the pigs: but no smarts. We had them by the shorts now.

"Gotta get you to the window, cat," I breathed. Eric obediently swung his legs over the edge of the bed.

"Why . . . window . . ." His head was lolling.

I unzipped my jacket to show him the rope wound around my waist. "I'm lowering you down to the ground. Help will be waiting there."

I slid up the aluminum sash, let in the night through the screen. Groovy. Like velvet. No noise.

Perch there, baby, I whispered. "I want the pig to come in and see you silhouetted, so I can take him from behind, dig?"

He nodded slowly. The injection was starting to take effect. It was my turn to squeeze his arm.

"Hang in there, baby."

I'd just gotten the night light switched off, had gotten behind the door, when I heard the pig's belatedly hurrying steps coming up the hall. Too late, you stupid fascist bastard, much too late.

A narrow blade of light stabbed at the room, widened to a rectangle. He didn't even come in fast, gun in hand, moving down and to the side as he should have. Just trotted in, a fat old porker to the slaughter. I heard his sharp intake of breath as he saw Eric.

"Hey! You! Get away from—"

I was on him from behind. Right arm around the throat, forearm grip, pull back hard while the left pushes on the back of the head. . . .

They go out easily with that grip, any of them. Good for disarming a sentry without using a knife, I had been taught. I hadn't wasted my Cuban sojourn chopping sugar cane like those student straights on the junkets from Canada. I feel nothing but contempt for *those* cats: they have not yet realized that destroying the fabric of society is the only thing left for us.

I dragged the unconscious pig quickly out the door, lowered his fat butt into his chair and stretched his legs out convincingly. Steady pulse. He'd come around in a few minutes; meanwhile, it actually would have been possible to just walk Eric down the fire stairs and out of the building.

For a moment I was tempted; but doing it that way wasn't in the plan. The plan called for the maximum effect possible, and merely walking Eric out would minimize it. Danzer's plan was everything.

Eric was slumped sideways against the window frame, mumbling sleepily. I pulled him forward, letting his head loll on my shoulder while I unhooked the screen and sent it sailing down into the darkness of the bushes flanking the concrete walk below. I could feel the coils of thin nylon around my waist, strong enough in their synthetic strength to lower him safely to the ground.

Jesus, he was one sweet guy. I paused momentarily to run my hand through his coarse, curly hair. There was sweat on his forehead. Last year he took my French exam for me so I could get my graduate degree. We'd met in old Prof Cecil's Western Civ course our junior year, and had been roomies until the end of grad school.

"I'm sorry, baby," I told his semiconscious, sweat-dampened face.

Then I let go and nudged, so his limp form flopped backward through the open window and he was gone, gone instantly, just like that. Three stories, head-first, to the concrete sidewalk. He hit with a sound like an egg dropped on the kitchen floor. A bad sound, man. One I won't soon forget.

The hall was dark and deserted as I stepped over the pig's outstretched legs. He'd be raising the alarm soon, but nobody except the other pigs would believe him. Not after the autopsy.

The first round of sirens came just after I had stuffed the thin surgical gloves down a sewer and was back in my car, pulling decorously away from the curb. The nylon rope, taken along only to convince Eric that I meant to lower him from the window, had been slashed into useless lengths and deposited in a curb-side trash barrel awaiting early morning collection.

On University Avenue, I turned toward an all-night hamburger joint that had a pay phone in the parking lot. I was, can you believe it, ravenous; but more than that, I was horny. I thought about that for a second, knowing I should feel sort of sick and ashamed at having a sexual reaction to the execution. But instead I felt . . . *transfigured*. Eric had been a political prisoner anyway; the pigs would have made sure he wouldn't have lived to come to trial. By his necessary death, *I* would be changing the entire history of human existence. *Me*. Alone.

And there was Liz over in the city, always eager, a receptacle in which I could spend my sexual excitement before she went off to teach. But first, Armand. So he could tell Danzer it was all right to print what we had discussed the night before.

Just thinking of that made me feel elated, because the autopsy would reveal the presence of that massive dose of truth serum I had needled into Eric before his death. And the Establishment news media would do the rest, hinting and probing and suggesting before our underground weeklies even hit the street with our charge against the fascists.

Waiting for Armand to pick up his phone, I composed our headline in my mind:

PIGS PUMP REVOLUTIONARY HERO FULL OF SCOPOLAMINE; HE DIVES FROM WINDOW RATHER THAN FINK ON THE MOVEMENT

Oh yes, man. Beautiful. Just beautiful. Watch for it.

I grew up around the Mississippi River marshes and wetlands of southern Minnesota because my Dad loved to fish and hunt. In college I tried unsuccessfully to use this background in a short story I called "Cacophony." Later I stole from "Cacophony" to put a Miami mobster into a midnight swamp where he had buried a man he had murdered. With, I hope, terrifying results.

QUIT SCREAMING

Morris would never forget that night, or Hausman, or the swamp. Hausman's sweat-runnelled face by lamplight, mouth strained open so far with his screaming that he looked like a basso profundo doing Don Basilio. And in the swamp, yellow-gray tendrils of mist groping up the twisted path and drifting over gnarled ancient roots under watery blue moonlight.

"Goddamnit," muttered Morris. This wasn't his kind of scene, he hadn't even shined his own shoes since he was ten.

And it had started so simply that afternoon, with a beach attendant saying Mr. Galatano wanted him at the hotel. Still in trunks and beach towel, he had gone into the office where Blachford fronted for the Family as manager of the vast resort hotel.

"You wanted to see me, Louis?"

Big Louie Galatano, alone in the room, smiled at him benignly. Not that anyone called him Big Louie to his face any more. It was Louis Galatano, Esq., now. Half a mil legit last year. George Morris knew, because he had made out Galatano's tax returns.

"Georgie baby, it's this creep of a bagman you okayed."

"Hausman?" Because he had been shacking up with Hausman's sister, Morris had gotten Hausman the position.

"Hausman. The take slipped a hundred a day when he took over West Palm Beach a month ago, but the bookies' gross is still up."

Morris was genuinely shocked. "He's been diverting funds?"

"Right. Rat-holing."

"What . . . are you going to do? His sister . . ."

"Not me, Georgie baby. What are *you* gonna do?"

Morris could remember the feel of sweat starting out on his bare skin under the huge, bright woolly beach towel. Cold sweat now, as he staggered up the path. How could he have taken a wrong turn after sinking the faceless, canvas-wrapped body in the swamp?

The fog had thickened, become almost palpable. Could he cut out a circle, lift it away to peer through at reality? Reality. Hang onto that. Galatano in the plush office, waving a drink with one hairy paw as he talked.

"You brought him in, Georgie baby, you take him out. We figger a month, half-a-gee a week, that's two thou. We want it back. From him, Georgie baby—or from you." He smiled, thick lips curving back to show expensively capped teeth, eyes mackerel-dead. "Time you got your feet wet in the operational end anyway, kid."

"But, Louis, I—"

The big left hand, the one with the cigar in it, rocked his head so hard to the right that for an instant Morris thought he would throw up. Galatano's right hand hadn't even slopped any of the drink it was holding. For that moment, Morris hated him. It was the first time that Big Louie's veneer had cracked to show the gutter underneath.

"Mr. Galatano to you right now, baby. You're in trouble, get it? You brought him in."

"But . . . Mr. Galatano, I'm . . . an accountant, not a—a—"

Big Louie's face softened. He put down his drink to lay a fatherly arm across the younger man's shoulders.

"Sure, kid. That's reasonable. I'm giving you two of the boys, Slim and Benny. Use the fishing shack down by the canal." He stopped at the door and beamed at Morris. "Okay, kid? Tonight. I want him *out* get me? Right out."

Out. Well, Hausman was out. In the swamp now, faceless from the blowtorch. Morris had suggested that little item for the fingers as a way of getting back the two thousand dollars so he wouldn't have to pony it up himself, but it had ended abruptly.

Behind him, down the path which he had climbed, was a thin yellow glow. Around him the wet stink of swamp rot, but hidden by a twist of the path, a lantern—another human being. Someone to direct him from this morass. Unless . . .

Morris paused suddenly. Moisture had formed on his face, even the moon seemed gray and muffled and old. The fog was thicker. Unless Hausman had come back to . . .

Knock it off. Hausman was dead, his face burned off by the blowtorch. Faceless. Sure a hell of a way to go, but his own fault. When Morris had started on his other hand, Hausman had shrieked and jerked so that the full blast of the torch had struck him right in the face.

Morris checked his watch. Midnight. Jesus, he wished he was out of here. Should have let Slim and Benny take care of the body. But he had felt a sudden bravado, had wanted them to carry back to Big Louie the awed word that Morris was tough—tough as they come. Shacking with the guy's sister but in the push . . .

The sodden rumple of fallen leaves sent him leaping back like a scalded cat so a dead branch gouged his back and his elbow struck agonizingly into a tree's rough bark. He opened his mouth to shout. From the lower depths of the swamp a huge distorted Hausman materialized in a rubber rain hat and rubber cape and . . .

Morris let the scream die unuttered. Not Hausman. Just a man made monstrous by the rain cape fastened at the throat and glistening dully where the thin blade of light from his old-fashioned lantern was honed against the rubber. The man was slogging steadily up the path in cumbersome gun boots turned down and then folded up again like the boots of the old buccaneers who had once habited the swamp. He would have gone by unheeding if Morris had not spoken.

"Hey you, Jack! Hold it a second."

The shadowy figure paused, then turned slowly to stare into the gloom under the oak tree where Morris cowered. Morris straightened up, angry with himself. He was glad his voice had been rough.

"What do you want, friend?" asked the swamp man.

Talk about voices. The raw muffled tones coming from the shadow under the rain hat were like pus from a wound. Glittering redly above the stubbly silver-shot beard were the eyes of a weasel as it snakes after a rabbit . . .

"I took a wrong path somehow. I want to get back to the canal." The man stank. Reeked. Swamp man, probably had a bath every six months or something.

"The canal? Boat canal?"

"Yeah. Where the fishing shack is." Where Slim and Benny were waiting with the car.

"Step out so's a man can see your face, friend."

As the swamp man spoke, a bittern boomed hollowly

down beyond the tangled live oaks of the swamp. His voice blended curiously with the cannoning of the bird. Then his hand moved against the lantern, opening it to impale Morris in a shaft of yellow light which shone off expensive shoes, a smart summer-weight suit and a pastel patterned shirt—all of them wet and stained and muddy now.

"Been down buryin' a body or somethin'?" Then high cackling loon-like laughter. Loons—big purple birds with white-spotted breasts, laughing dementedly in the dusk. "Anyway, you sure dress purty. Lost, y'say?"

"Listen, Jack," snapped Morris, hoping to steady himself with his voice "if you don't want to help—"

The man cackled again, but pointed back down the path into the drifting whisps of fog.

"See down there? How she branches? Now, what you do . . ."

Morris stepped closer to look. He could remember no fork in the path. In proximity the man smelled of the swamp-decayed things like a dead carp's insides when you stepped hard on it and burst open its bloated belly. The stench made Morris recoil. His foot tipped over the lantern. As it went out, the last gleam sprang up directly into the swamp man's face.

Morris reared back, screaming like a fire-trapped stallion.

The man had no face.

Morris screamed again under the wan moonglow as bear-hugging arms closed around him in obscene embrace. The thing that should have been a face mumbled against his.

"Quit screaming, don't do no good. Don't you want . . . faceless . . ."

Morris sank an unpracticed but panic-driven fist into the

tarry dough where the face should have been. The swamp man staggered, Morris twisted, jerked, was free, away.

Saw grass slashed his ankles vindictively, a million tiny blades lacing his legs with blood. His shoe caught a snarl of grass and hurled him headlong into a stale soupy socket between two hummocks. He staggered to his feet, splashed on, wheezing, as he worked deeper into the swamp. Behind, loon-like laughter from the demented creature. He risked a look over his shoulder. Behind him only shredded whisps of fog drifting back into place. No faceless creature. No path.

Had he imagined it all? Lost his way in a frenzy fear?

Morris splashed on because he had no other way to go, each movement making broad ripples on the oily water under the muffling smoke. Around him the smell of rot, ahead smooth-sleek water moccasins undulating, behind dead garfish speared and thrown back floating.

Quit screaming, the thing had said.

Imagination, fear-triggered. Had to be. He had used the same words to Hausman after he'd finished with the first hand. "Quit screaming. Nobody can hear you except us anyway." Enjoying himself, then.

Not now. Scummy green water under a dying gray-green moon. Ahead, grassy hummocks, water around them, slogging through, mid-calf, ankle deep, finally unwatered spongy loam underfoot holding his weight. He sank down, breath grating in tortured lungs. Off with a shoe to squelch out bits of bark and watercress. Other shoe.

He must have imagined it all, must have floundered away from the path in sheer animal panic. All right now.

But what was the stuff smeared tar-like and viscid across his knuckles? The knuckles he had swung at the apparition's face? Without thinking, Morris sniffed them. The stench bent him over, spewing violently, left him spent and panting. His panic drove him to scrabble his hands in the inky water, scrubbing the knuckles with bark until they bled. But the reek finally was gone.

Where was he? A frog carrunked in front of him. Crickets sawed tenor over the base section, soprano mosquitoes whined their toneless melody. Nightjars swooped and wheeled black above him in pursuit of night insects. Where? And what time?

Midnight.

But the faceless thing had come from the swamp at midnight. Easy, man. Watch stopped. From the swamps of his mind, rather.

The moon had reappeared, dimmer, lower, like candle seen through gauze. Fog only waist high now, a drifting blanket never still, sometimes puffing up in slow seethes like dry ice. Faceless creatures . . .

No, goddamnit, knock it off. Mind morasses only.

Long bent marsh grass spurned underfoot as he staggered on. Indistinct moisture—green tapering ends tucked down to tiny roots, a million saw blades along its million edges. Tangled thorny bushes, live massive oaks, bannered with gray streamers of tattered Spanish moss. Dim tree trunks like twisted columns.

Morris tensed. His swamp-attuned senses had detected a far-off, alien sound. Alien to the swamp.

Yes. Again.

He was running toward the hum of auto tires on a blacktop road. *There!* Between sentinel cypresses gaunt in gray water, the pinpoint flicker of headlights, instantly gone. Running—galloping rather—sprawling and slipping, now in stinging grass, over extended clutching roots. Shoe gone, no matter, hobbling on with wrenched ankle, no matter. Mud slurping up between his toes through tattered sock, no matter. The road was there.

Gibbering, he dodged through a narrow belt of hardwoods to firm ground, heedless of cottonmouths, *sprong!* full-tilt into a barbed-wire fence. He was hurled back by its springy resilient lengths, lashed across cheek and chest, no matter. Rolling heedless under the strands to tumble full-length into a ditch. Fetid. Stinking. Terror's last try, clutching at his mind, but free now. Clawing his way up an embankment to the levee road.

Safe. Black top under feathered moonglow. Cool breeze balming; ego busy to turn him from fleeing animal to man once more. Hausman gone. Swamp behind him. Safe.

Around a bend in the road came a swelling hum of auto, then a flicker of headlight. He stepped out, semaphoring wildly. If the car wouldn't stop . . .

But it did. Brake linings *eeered* unevenly against clutching drums. Morris was running before the car stopped. The driver reached across to push open the passenger's door, and Morris stuck his head in to tumble out words while his back crawled for a final time in fear of swamp things.

"Fishing for big-mouths . . . lost way . . . wet and muddy . . . need . . ."

"Hell, that's okay, hop in."

It was an old car but looked like a Caddy with air and power everything to Morris. Despite a broken dome light, he could see that the driver was a slim young man his own age, his own build, with a gray suit and rakish narrow-brimmed hat with a jaunty feather in the band.

"Sorry I went by you so far, sport, but hitchhikers out here . . ."

"I—I know. Damned nice of you to—to stop at all—"

The car jerked ahead, picked up speed with a thunderous rattle of a bad muffler, and Morris relaxed—or thought he did. The swamp was gone, back there with its faceless Hausman and faceless hallucination, but he found he was trembling uncontrollably.

"Hey, you're all wet sport! Let me turn up the heater."

"J—Just reaction." Morris patted sodden pockets for a cigarette, teeth clenched firm to keep from chattering. Welcome heat began coursing though the car. The driver shook two super-kings into his trembling hands.

"Here. One for later, too." He gestured at the dashboard lighter and went on, "You're a mess, sport. Maybe a doctor—"

"*No!*" He made himself relax as he pushed in the lighter. "It's just that I had a hell of an experience down there. This guy . . ."

He paused, wishing he hadn't started the story. It was too new, still too real. And with the heater warming him, he seemed to catch a vagrant whisp of swamp stink clinging to his clothes. He shuddered. Probably permeating them. He would burn them back at the hotel. He . . .

"What about this guy?" asked the driver.

"He . . . well, he had a lantern. I was asking directions, and I—by accident, I kicked it over. As it went out . . ."

He shuddered. He definitely had brought the sickening reek of the swamp man into the car with him. Or was he imagining that now? In sudden panic he wondered if something like that could permeate the flesh itself? Christ! He'd hit the hotel sauna, the steam room, get a massage—anything to . . .

The lighter popped. Morris jammed it against his cigarette and dragged deeply. Nothing. Lighter dead. Goddamnit! Instead of soothing smoke, he had sucked that damned stink into his lungs.

The driver dipped into his coat pocket again. "I always forget that thing is burned out. Here. Try these."

Morris fumbled out one of the old-fashioned wooden kitchen matches, scraped the head along the abrasive at the side of the box, hunched forward to light his cigarette with the welcome smell of sulphur momentarily killing the stench of swamp decay.

"So, you kicked over the lantern, sport. Then what happened?"

Morris dragged in blessed smoke. "So the light hit him in the face and he—he didn't have a face."

The driver jerked around to stare at him, wide-eyed, as Morris raised the match to wave it out. For a split second its light sprang up under the brim of the jaunty hat.

"Like me?" the driver inquired pleasantly.

The car swerved wildly across the narrow levee blacktop as bear-hugging arms closed around Morris in an obscene embrace. Morris reared back against the door, screaming, felt the latch give behind him . . .

A cruising sheriff's deputy found him just after dawn, wandering on the levee road at the edge of the swamp. He and the tattered rags of his clothing reeked fetidly. He was wet and muddy and exhausted, and from the multiple minor bruises on his body he must have fallen from a slow-moving auto. Apart from the bruises and a wrenched ankle, however, he was physically unharmed.

But when he saw the deputy, he started screaming.

He still is.

While a private eye, I was sent to Palm Springs to find an errant debtor and repossess her car. I later used this experience to tell the tale of a hired killer on an assignment that tests his contemptuous belief that dying is always swift and easy for those he murders. This was my second published story, written in Tahiti, sold while I was in the Army at the Pentagon.

KILLER MAN

The stewardess came by checking reservations.

"Your name please, sir."

"Simmons," said Falkoner. He was lean and dark, with long-fingered hands shaped like a piano player's and cool gray eyes that observed almost everything. A thin white scar running across his chin made his otherwise pleasant face sullen. In his shoulder holster was a .357 Magnum on a cut-down frame and in his bleak heart was death. Falkoner was a professional murderer.

During the thirty-five minute flight from Los Angeles the lone woman huddled across the aisle aroused his melancholy contempt. She wore a cheap brown hat and had an old straw purse on the seat next to her. Updrafts over the rim of the desert made her tight fists whiten with strain and her eyes burn with fear. She was disgusting: he knew dying was swift and easy.

A slight sandy-haired man took his arm as he left the plane at Palm Springs and said: "Did Mr. David send you down?" His voice was soft and intimate and he wore a red and green sports shirt, khaki pants, and open sandals.

Looking him over, Falkoner nodded coolly. Little men who did not deal in the two great realities of life and death held scant interest for him.

"Fine. I'm Langly. My car's over here in the lot."

It was a blue and white 1957 Chrysler. On the blacktop road beyond the airport the sun was warm but the air dry and fresh; scraggly clumps of dusty green vegetation spotted the flat desert like regimented billiard balls on a giant yellow table. They passed a man and woman on horseback, wearing riding breeches, who waved gaily. A Cadillac Eldorado roared by like an escaped rocket, manned by two bleached blondes goggled with bright-rimmed sunglasses.

"Where's the woman?" asked Falkoner.

"She's got a shack in a date grove near Rancho Mirage— it's a new section this side of Palm Desert."

"Works?"

"Mex place in Palm Desert. She tells fortunes, goes to work at five—she'll be home now." Langly's voice tingled and his bright eyes sparkled ripely. "I guess Mr. David wants her pretty bad, huh? I just notified Los Angeles last night, and you're here from 'Frisco today to—"

"Let's go out to her place."

Langly drove swiftly as if stung by Falkoner's abruptness. They passed the plush Thunderbird Club and turned left onto a dirt road before the Shadow Mountain Club. Dry clouds of tan dust swirled out behind them.

"When word came she'd left Scottsdale I thought she might try it here—the country's a lot the same. Then I spotted her at the Mex place from her photo and—"

"Are we close?"

Langly drove across an old wash beyond which the date groves started.

"Next road to the right, first house on the left," he said.

His voice was sharp and piqued. "Only house."

"Okay. Drive past."

Down the narrow roadway Falkoner saw the tail of a black Mercury station wagon protruding from behind a palm tree. The shack was hidden by trees.

"That her Merc?"

"Yes. A '55 Monterey with wood paneling. A beauty."

After a moment of thought Falkoner said: "Turn around up here and let me off at the roadway. Then you go back to town."

As he followed directions the other's actions had a slightly feminine quality. Falkoner got out, walked around the car, and dropped a sealed envelope through the window into Langly's lap. The envelope crinkled.

"What sort of work do you do?" Falkoner asked.

"I've been parking cars at one of the clubs." Then the voice got malicious; excitement made it almost lisp. "But I did good work on this and I'm going to make sure Mr. David knows about it and about how you've treated me."

"Stick to parking cars, nance," Falkoner replied. Leaning very close he added confidentially: "You've got a leaky face."

In his steady eyes Langly saw death's cold scrutiny. He rammed the *drive* button hurriedly and the Chrysler swept him away down the dusty road.

Palm fronds tickled the roof drily and something gnawed with cautious haste under the sagging wooden porch. Falkoner's shoes made cat sounds as he crossed to the screen door. After knocking on the frame he cupped his eyes to peer into the living room. The linoleum was so old it was worn almost white. Across the room sagged a beaten-down green couch, in one corner a red easy chair that looked almost new. There were three straight-backed chairs and one leg of the wooden table in the center of the floor had been cracked and stapled. A plaque reading GOD BLESS OUR HOME decorated one wall.

Before he could call, Genevieve came through the inner doorway. She was as tall as he, nearly six feet, her face fine-featured: straight nose, high cheekbones, thin hungry lips. A red silk scarf was knotted loosely around her neck and her striking figure was displayed by a tight black dress. There were three hairpins in her mouth and her hands were smoothing her hair.

"Yes?" Her voice was husky.

The screen door was unlocked so Falkoner stepped in. When the light touched his features she went stark white and her mouth dropped the hairpins. She ran against him, slanted dark eyes smoky with terror, but he pushed her back.

"Rather a come-down, Genevieve," he said.

He went through the inner doorway to see a small dirty kitchen with dishes piled in the sink, and a bedroom with a double bed that looked as if two large animals had been fighting on it. The room had a close, intimate smell. As he donned a pair of thin gray gloves he let Genevieve's voice draw him back to the front room.

"What does he want with me? He—whoever killed Max . . . I didn't see who killed Max."

"If you hadn't left Arizona he might have believed you."

"I got tired of the stinking desert and the stinking men with only one thing on their stinking minds."

Falkoner raised his eyebrows. "The men at the Mex place are different? The desert here is different?"

"I had to eat." Her mouth made the next word a curse. "Men. You and Mr. David and all the rest. Money and power and women, that's all you want." Then the strength left her and her hands crawled up the black dress like broad white spiders to her bosom.

"Isn't he ever going to let me live in peace?" she whispered.

Falkoner asked: "Did you really think he could let you live at all?" His quick hands closed around her throat like an act of love.

She scrabbled wildly at the iron-hard forearms, reached for his eyes, tried to kick him. She was strong, but the piano-player fingers possessed all the immeasurable strength of evil. A chair was overturned. They went around the table in a slow grotesque dance like cranes mating. He drove her down on the couch and kneed her viciously. The thrashing body, the smell of sweat and perfume aroused him: it was a pity there was no time to have her before she died. A great pity.

Her face darkened, her movements became erratic, lost volition, ceased. Finally her tongue, pink as a baby's thumb, came out of one corner of her mouth and spittle ran down her cheek. There was a muted sound like cloth tearing. She sprawled under him in a lewd doll-pose of surrender, eyes staring beyond him into the infinite horror of death.

From a payphone at a gas station on South Palm Drive, Falkoner reversed the charges to a Tuxedo exchange number in San Francisco. While awaiting his connection he placidly smoked a cigarette. The operator said:

"I have a collect call for anyone from a Mr. Simmons in Palm Springs. Will you accept the charges?"

A flat voice answered: "Put him on."

Falkoner ground out his cigarette against the window of the booth and said "Yes" into the receiver. There was no response so he hung up, paid for his gas, and left Palm

Springs, driving west across the desert on U.S. 101. At U.S. 99 he went north to Colton, cut across to U.S. 66 on a dirt road, and again pointed the Mercury at the far thin glow of Los Angeles. He counted bugs as they squashed against the windshield, and at nine o'clock ate Mexican food in a small adobe diner. It had been a clean hit: her body, wrapped in a blanket, was stuffed in the spare tire well under the floor section of the Mercury, and a suitcase full of her personal things rode beside him. Yet he lacked the usual drained empty peace. Around midnight some instinct made him pull in at a motel near Glendora, two hours from the city.

The single row of white cottages was neat and freshly painted; each unit had a covered carport with a door leading directly inside. Above the first cabin a large red neon sign proclaimed MOTEL with *vacancy* underneath in smaller pink letters. After he had rung the bell twice, the office light went on and an old man with a sour face like the taste of lemon came out of the back room rubbing his eyes. An old-fashioned nightshirt covered bowed legs.

"Is your last unit in the line empty?"

Clicking his false teeth together, he leaned past Falkoner as if to make sure there was a last unit. He smelled sourly of sleep.

"Yep."

"Fine. I have trouble sleeping if I can hear traffic passing. How much?"

"Five bucks."

"Commercial rates."

"Well—four, then."

Falkoner did the other careful things the years had taught him: wrote 'Simmons' on the register in a slanting backhand script that was not his own, mixed up the license number in a way that could have been accidental, and took

Genevieve's suitcase with him before locking the car. Opening the motel room door, he breathed deeply; orange groves flanking the highway made the air faintly sweet. Maybe it was getting to him. Five years ago he'd never considered the possibility of anything going wrong. *Tomorrow I'll dump her with Dannelson,* he thought, *and maybe get lined up with a little piece. I've been living like a monk lately.*

"Let me talk to Danny," Falkoner said, rubbing his eyes and cursing the gray fingers of smog reaching out from Los Angeles. Sunday morning traffic made it difficult to hear.

"Who's calling?"

"Falkoner."

"Falkoner? I'm sorry, Mr. Dannelson is out."

Falkoner squeezed the receiver tightly. The palm of his hand had gone sweaty.

"Is Dannelson out or did he say he was out?" he asked.

"Mr. Dannelson is out."

There were muttered angry words, a click, and Dannelson's voice came jovially over the wire.

"Hello, Jack? That damned fool didn't get your name right. Listen, boy, S.F. said you had a parcel for us. Where in hell are you?"

Falkoner hung up abruptly, returned to the car, and tuned the radio to a ten o'clock newscast. It carried the item for which Dannelson's clumsiness had prepared him.

Palm Springs police were investigating the disappearance and possible murder of Genevieve Ostroff, fortune-teller at the Green Cactus bar in Palm Desert. Two boys playing near her house had seen a man carrying what looked like a blanket-wrapped body to her black station wagon. Investigating police had found no sign of violence and her clothes had been gone, but there had been over seven hundred dollars in small bills under the paper lining of a dresser drawer. After the first newscast Chester Langly, parking lot attendant at the Blue Owl, had furnished the description of a man who had hitched a ride with him from the airport to a point near Genevieve's house. A man who had called himself Simmons.

Damn that fairy Langly, Falkoner thought. The police were easy, but Mr. David had given him the contract for Genevieve personally . . . now he was too dangerous to live. The word was already out: lucky Danny'd been so anxious. Los Angeles and Las Vegas and San Diego—probably Tucson and El Paso, too, because they'd figure him to try for Mexico. No place to run: and to run would mean admitting to himself he was afraid. Suddenly his pale morose face cleared. *What if he went back to San Francisco after Mr. David?* That was it. It was what they should expect of Jack Falkoner.

The maid had finished his room. He paid at the office for a week in advance, then carried the heavy unwieldy package that was Genevieve in through the side entrance and dumped it on the bed.

A light blue 1955 Ford pulled out behind him on the traffic circle at Bakersfield. The tail job was clumsy. Falkoner drove fast: this boy mustn't have time to get to a phone. On the new freeway north of Delano he suddenly floored the accelerator and squealed into the right-angle turn for the Earlimart overpass, swung over to old U.S. 99, and pulled up in front of a little general store he had remembered. It was the run-down country crossroads sort of place occasionally surviving in the San Joaquin Valley. The sort of place to do what had to be done.

A short man wearing dirty overalls and chewing a large cud of tobacco came out.

"Fill it up—regular," said Falkoner.

He waited in the store by the vegetable counter. Three dirty bare-footed children slammed through the screen door and began noisily clamoring at the candy counter like puppies worrying a bone. A tall faded lady in a washed-out dress came from the bowels of the store to scream harsh threats at them.

When the blue Ford rounded the corner and braked sharply, Falkoner went out the door and around behind the store to the primitive outdoor restrooms. Lattice works into which thick vines had grown flanked the entrance. He slammed the lean-to door loudly, stepped out of sight behind the vines, and took the Magnum from its shoulder holster. Feet scuffed in the dust and foliage rustled. Door hinges squeaked cautiously.

The young red-haired man had freckles and a homely face and a switchblade knife in one broad paw. As he turned from the empty shanty, puzzled, Falkoner stepped around the lattice work and slammed the Magnum down on his hand. Pimples of sweat popped out on his hard young face. The knife fell. He snatched clumsily for the Magnum with his left hand, breathing hoarsely, his eyes already sick with the sure frightful knowledge of defeat.

Falkoner's gun rammed him in the stomach, bending him over; then it clipped him across the back of the neck and knocked him to his knees. A knee driven into his freckled face upset him against the wall. The Magnum struck his bright hair with a sound like a wet rag slapping concrete. He tipped forward on his face and was still.

Falkoner dragged him around the corner of the shanty and killed him.

The short man was still cleaning bugs from the Mercury's windshield when the blue Ford dug out and sped past the gas pumps.

Night had darkened San Francisco when Jack Falkoner took the down ramp off the freeway at Seventh, crossed Market, and went up Larkin. He drove over the hill to Pacific, turned right, crossed over the Broadway tunnel on Mason, and parked the Ford. His hands shook a little as he checked the Magnum: going after Mr. David was something like going up against God.

Turning downhill at Glover, a narrow one-block alley, he walked on the right-hand side, crossed over, and came up the other side breathing heavier from the incline. There were no cars he knew, no people at all, so he turned in at an ornate wooden gate and climbed a series of stone steps. In less than a minute he had opened the heavy oak door with a small metal pick and was prowling the five-room apartment. His rubber soles made no sound on the polished floors and thick carpets. On Sundays Mr. David and the girl he kept there usually watched Ed Sullivan, but tonight the apartment was empty.

I can wait, Falkoner thought as he returned to the Ford, and slid in behind the wheel.

A round hard object poked the base of his neck and a smooth voice said:

"Hands on the head, Sweets, and slide over slow."

Strangely, he thought of his first hit. *It had been in a car like this and the man had said. "I'm not afraid of you."* He did not say anything. A dark figure came erect in the back seat and another crossed the street swiftly to get in under the wheel and hold a gun on Falkoner while the first one took the Magnum. *Later the man had cried and babbled and even prayed. Falkoner had been much younger then and had laughed before shooting him in the back of the head.*

A long black sedan drifted around the corner and crawled up behind them. It was remarkably like an undertaker's car. When the man at the wheel flipped his lights twice the Ford pulled out. The sedan followed. They took Pine to Presidio, cut over to Balboa, and drove out through the dark still Avenues decorously, like a funeral procession. Falkoner's head ached and he felt sick to his stomach. When he looked at the unfamiliar face of the driver, the man in the back seat said, "Don't try it, Sweets." The driver stayed hunched over with both hands on the wheel. They would not let him smoke a cigarette.

Surf grumbled against the concrete breakwaters as the Ford turned left onto the Great Highway at Playland on the Beach. Only a few rides and stalls were open, for a chill March mist had rolled in off the Pacific. The wipers monotonously sucked haze from the windshield. After several miles they swung in facing the ocean on a wide dirt lot where neckers parked on moonlit nights. The sedan drew up behind them, parallel to the highway, with dimmed lights. There were no other cars. A tangled hedge of dark twisted cypress, bent and gnarled by the incessant wind, screened them from the houses beyond the highway.

The doorhandle felt cold and slippery to Falkoner's fingers. Bitter words flooded his mouth like bile and his lips bled keeping them in: *Jack Falkoner is not afraid, Jack Falkoner is not afraid. . . .* He flung open the door and threw himself at the opening. Behind him something plopped twice. Eyes staring in disbelief, he fell dizzily out of the half-open door and crashed down on one shoulder. He tried to say something, he wanted to say it, it was important: the whole significance of his life had been only death. He had meant no more than a casual accident or a mild epidemic that snuffs out a few people by blind chance. If they would just give him a little time for change, another month for living. . . . Before he could ask, orange flame spurted and lead ripped his throat, slamming his head into the dirt with an ineluctable finality.

"Pay me," chortled Mr. David in high good humor. The sedan had turned by Fleishaker Zoo and was threading through an expensive residential district on broad Sloat Avenue.

The man in the back seat with him was dressed in a camel's hair coat and had crisp wavy hair receding from his forehead. He had once been a lawyer but had been disbarred. With obvious reluctance he took a hundred dollar bill from his wallet and handed it to his employer.

"I still don't see how you knew he'd come up here. I thought one of the boys along the border would tag him."

Mr. David chuckled richly. He wore too much cologne in a vain effort to disguise the constant odor of perspiration that clung to his obese body like the smell of bad cooking. His heavy features were shadowed by his hat brim.

"Psychology, Norman, psychology. Jack wasn't afraid of me or the Organization or Old Nick himself. It was his sort of stunt, to try and take me with him. I'm sorry about Red, though. I told him to be careful but you know how kids are."

"How can you be so sure Falkoner got him?"

"The Ford. Jack would never have had that car if Red was alive, that's for sure. And Jack was a bad one, at that."

"I like 'em bad," put in the man in the middle of the front seat. He was removing a steel cylinder from the muzzle of his .32, his deadly hands fondling the revolver with the quick and supple movements of a musician fingering his guitar.

"And you can't tell me Sweets wasn't scared. I saw his face when he went under."

Mr. David delicately shifted his ponderous bulk and belched. His weight made the seat coils creak slightly.

"We'll never know now, will we?" he demanded with unction. As the car stopped for the light on 19th Avenue he added: "Take a left here, Freddie. I've got a date with a new girl."

Down toward Playland, a motorcycle siren whined thinly, like a short-haired mongrel in cold weather. The chilled huddle of people could see the flat pink glow of its close-set red eyes coming up at them through the fog. Moaning wind tore their breaths away in gray tatters. Occasional cars whipped past, wet tires hissing on the shiny pavement. By the white empty glare of their patrol car spotlight, two wet-tunicked policemen resembled grave robbers rolling bodies as they lifted Falkoner's corpse by one shoulder to see if it bore any life. On his face, almost ferocious in its intensity, was frozen an immutable expression of pure terror.

For a science-fiction anthology they were editing, Chelsea Quinn Yarbro and Tom Scortia assigned common themes to pairs of writers, one female, one male. The late Miriam Allen de Ford and I drew: "After watching the televised torture-murder of his/her lover, the protagonist must devise a communication system for the revolutionary underground in a society tyrannized by complete electronic surveillance." I used the then-novel theory of black holes to tell of an astronaut stranded in an alternate universe who finds love and hate and a burning desire for revenge.

FAULTY REGISTER

Up from the Ghetto to the Stars. No shit, that was one of the headlines when I was picked for the mission by NASA. The first spade on Mars, from rats in the cradle to my black ass lighting up the firmaments. Something else entirely.

But we missed.

Dig it, man, whatever you look like who's reading this, in whatever millennium of whatever crazy universe you inhabit: we missed Mars. Which makes it a hell of a drive to the next off-ramp.

"Honey. Wake up."

"Huh?"

"Wake up." Clemmie's voice. "You're having that dream again."

I sat up in bed, nude and sweating. Moonlight through the open window silvered Clemmie's dark and lovely breasts. Of course I'm talking about *this* Clemmie. Here. This not-quite-Clemmie in this not-quite California in this not-quite. . . .

"It isn't any dream, lady. I'm *not* the Zeke Dooley you think I am."

She put a hand on me. I reacted—hell, I'm only human. She giggled. "You *act* like Zeke, honey."

I spent half an hour acting like Zeke, while she acted like Clemmie. *My* Clemmie, back in *my* California, same flashing dark eyes full of bawdy promise, same smooth brown hide turning feverish under my caresses. So why *not* Clemmie?

Because, goddammit, we missed Mars.

Three of us on the flight: Major Long, USAF, mission captain; Jackson, USN, astronaut; Dooley, civilian, computer engineer, token black. Long and Jackson are dead; I'm alive because I was back checking out the reentry vehicle. No memorable last words; they'd never incise on a tombstone what was said back and forth over the intercom—even if there were anything left to put under it.

"Son of a bitch, anyway." Long, big sandy-haired cat with an Indiana twang with, then, only irritation in his voice. "We've lost contact with Houston Control."

"We've also lost Mars," said Jackson. Concern in his voice.

I thought they were putting me on because I wasn't a regular astronaut, merely an election-year token. But there was a sudden frightened awe in Jackson's voice.

"Mars is just . . . gone. As if a cloud has drifted between us and it. But . . . there can't be any clouds where there isn't any atmosphere. Can there?"

"Everything's dead," said Long in a terribly conversational voice. "Everything's just gone—"

Tremendous slam of naked force, a rending of metals, the reentry vehicle with me encapsulated inside was ripped out of the womb of the mothership like a foetus aborted in a high-speed crash. I was staring at the deformed remains a dozen feet, three hundred yards, a mile away as we moved on divergent courses. The spaceship became a silver pencil, stretched to a thread like molten glass, was a ray of light, then was rammed down into zero volume, into infinite density. Gone, through the black hole into the time-space singularity which I had somehow escaped.

"I just don't *understand!*" cried Clemmie doggedly over post-coital coffee. She wanted me to be *her* Ezechiel Dooley. "If you're not him, then—"

"Then he's a pinhead of crushed matter somewhere else, or has taken my place in *my* universe—"

She burst out, "Oh, Zeke, see the medics! *Please! You are* Zeke, *my* Zeke, and—"

I was shaking my head.

"For one millisecond in time, Clemmie, our alternate universes brushed wings. And two spaceships, at the rims of their respective universes—"

"But how can two universes coexist without . . . without—"

"A universe is a vast closed system. So vast that no light can escape. So until they actually touched, neither would know that the other was there."

"Oh, Zeke!" she wailed.

Coffee cups dumped on the floor, hands all over each other. Only when our bodies were mated could she totally believe in me.

But she couldn't *disbelieve,* either. Clemmie's point was that *if* our universes were identical even if coexistent, then how did I know I was in a different world from my own in the first place? I tried to explain it as faulty register.

"See this picture?" I picked up the *TV Guide* from the

coffee table and pointed to the cover. "This required four separate color runs. One of them was just a little bit off, see? The color isn't just exactly where it's supposed to be in relation to the other three. In printing that's known as *faulty register.* Just a little blurred. Like this universe is to me . . . "

She was the only one I ever tried to convince. I'd learned something was wrong almost immediately, right after the press conference when they'd finished the reentry vehicle with me in it from the ocean. Until then, dig, I'd thought I'd somehow made it back to earth in some sort of amnesiac blackout which prevented me from remembering the solitary months of the return voyage.

It was General Harginson, Chief of Mission, who started it when I was back in the debriefing area.

"You made some remarkable statements out there, Dooley."

"I've had a remarkable experience."

He turned from the window of the small cell-like room. "Why did you refer to yourself as a black man, Dooley?"

Was this dude trying to put me on? I didn't have to take his sass, I was *civilian,* man.

"We can use Negro if you prefer, general. Colored if you're old-fashioned. Darkie if you're a Mormon. Maybe even spade, if you smile when you say it. But—"

He was shaking his head. "You know that all racial differences were ended by decree over a century ago."

I put my black arm up next to his white one. I also mentally rehearsed where the door was, just in case. He was into his sixties but he was big. If he got violent . . .

"Black . . . white. See, general? Simon Legree chasing little Liza across the ice floe?" I did a minstrel buck-and-wing, ended up on a knee with my hand out in the Jolson manner. "Mammy?"

"Men with different colored skins, Dooley?" It was the

general who had edged toward the safety of the door. "Unthinkable. Absolutely unthinkable."

Two extra weeks of medical tests looking for the loose screws. If it hadn't been that I was able to talk to Clemmie by intercom from the isolation trailer, see her through the thick glass seal, I'd have thought it was some sort of Rip Van Winkle jazz. You know, man, waking up twenty years later and all that. But the newspapers confirmed what the Harginson episode had already suggested. This *was* a world different from the one I'd left. No stories of international tensions. No race riots or prison breaks. No unemployment figures. No crime news.

And yet there was Clemmie, finally come to pick me up from the medical isolation and take me home. Goddammit, *my* Clemmie, you dig? Voice, face, eyes, *everything*. But *not* Clemmie. Couldn't be, because I was in the wrong place. After we'd embraced and kissed, I said, just to test the theory I'd started developing, "Let's drive through the ghetto on the way home."

She burst out laughing.

"I swear, Zeke, they should have kept you locked up for *another* two weeks. Ghetto! You know very well the decree against poverty is nearly a hundred years old—ever since they abolished capitalism—"

"Not a time warp," I said sadly. "Another universe."

Shot through a goddam wormhole from one universe to another. Coexisting, similar, but not mine. Clemmie stopped the car in front of a double for my own familiar house. Her big black eyes looked at me in sudden solemnity.

"Zeke, you been having fun with me, and from what those space agency people said you had fun with them, too. But . . . Zeke . . . not when we're alone, honey. It . . . gives me a scary feeling."

"What color are we, Clemmie? You and me?"

"Color?" She started to giggle. "*People* color."

A honky woman was wheeling a baby carriage by on the sidewalk. It was getting on toward dusk, but there was enough light to see *that*.

"Are we the same color she is?"

Clemmie looked. She nodded, sort of solemn-like. I sighed.

"Then there's no difference between her and us."

"There's no difference between anybody and anybody, Zeke. Why . . . why, if differences between people were allowed, that would mean there were *inequalities* between people. And that would be—"

"Yeah." I'd been hearing the word a good deal during my debriefing, so I used it. "Unthinkable."

So here I was, man, where they'd just about solved 'em all. Racism. Poverty. The Protestant work-ethic. Crime.

No racism, because it was unthinkable that men could be born with any inequalities between them. Dig? No poverty, because there was no private property. No unemployment, because everybody who worked, worked for the state. But you didn't really have to work. You could do your own thing. No pigs, of course, because there were no jails to put people in and nobody to arrest anyway, because there weren't any criminals.

"What if I went next door and zonked old what's-his-face—Jennings—on toppa his bald pate?"

"*That* wouldn't be a crime!" Clemmie laughed. "That would be the unvolitional action of a clinically disturbed man. You'd need help—"

"So would Jennings."

Not the point, dig? The state would take care of *both* of

us—or Jennings' widow if it came to that. He would be suc-
cored, I would be cured of my anti-social illness.

"Cured how?" I asked cautiously.

"Therapy, of course." She giggled at me. "Sometimes I
almost believe you *are* from a different universe. . . ."

Clinically disturbed. If you did anything criminal you
were ill, not evil—because where there is no personal responsibility there can be no morality. Or immorality.

The perfect society, man. Racism, crime, guilt, all unthinkable. Heaven on earth.

Except for the Hour of Release.

It was the night after we'd had that discussion about
whapping old man Jennings next door on the head. I suppose that was what got her thinking about it, but anyway
Clemmie turned on the big color TV. I'd had it on a time or
two in the afternoon, but it'd been what you could expect
when a creative enterprise is being run by state bureaucrats.
This was different.

"Hey! Cops and robbers!" I sat down on the couch beside Clemmie and put an arm around her shoulders. It was
a chase sequence, with the heroine being threatened by . . .

"It's the Hour of Release," she said in a hushed voice.
She had sweat on her upper lip. "They're going to get her."

"If they do, it'll be the first time in the history of TV."

"Get her," Clemmie repeated.

The girl was a slender fox in her twenties, the baddies
were like out of an old Nazi movie, big and blond and hard-
faced and wearing trenchcoats. Industrial sort of streets, but
then I realized it was inside a deserted factory. The chick
was a good actress, really terrified-seeming, throwing these
wide-eyed looks over her shoulders. But the baddies knew
their business. I settled down for the hero to show up.

"Get her get her get her." Clemmie was almost chanting it.

Man, they got her. I mean, they really *got* her. One of them finally trapped her, and then suddenly came up with this long thin knife and slashed her right across the face with it. She went down, yelling. Suddenly the second one was tearing her panties off.

I tried to keep the shock out of my face. The one with the knife was *banging* her, right there on the TV screen! Banging her in fifty million homes!

"Do it do it do it," chanted Clemmie.

He not only did it, he held her so the other one could do it, too. Finally the second cat started moaning and thrashing around on her and then, through clenched teeth, got out a single word you could hear even through the noise she was making.

"Now!" he said.

The knife plunged into her throat. Her screams cut off into wet gurgles. Blood sprayed over the two rapists, so realistically that it made me feel sick. I looked over at Clemmie, mouth open to say something unbelieving, and then I *really* felt sick. She was making it, too, right along with the guy mounted on the fox in the movie.

She caught my eyes on her, suddenly put her head down and the tears came, a real case of hysterics.

"They murdered her!" she screamed. "Oh, I'm so ashamed!"

I finally caught it. Hour of Release.

That's right, man, it had to come out somewhere. Nobody responsible, nobody guilty—they'd been able to *logically* convince people that nothing was forbidden, nothing was wrong, but something inside the people still didn't believe it.

Hitler tried the same thing with the Master Race. Just a matter of logistics, transport X units here, dispose of Y units there. The Nazis really *believed,* man. But when the Allies were coming in, they tried to obliterate the camps. It was more than just fear. It was guilt. Shame.

Here, the Hour of Release. Revel in innocence destroyed. Enjoy vicarious rape, murder, torture through the actors. Come out cleansed, released, purged.

Get an orgasm out of it, on the house.

To my shame, Clemmie got a second orgasm out of me, on the floor in front of the now-dark TV twenty minutes after her hysterics had stopped. It was the closest to rape I've ever had done to me.

"I'm just sleepy," she said in a sweet sated voice against the hollow of my throat when I mentioned my shame afterwards.

I sat up on the rug. "How . . . often do they run that damned thing?"

"Eleven to midnight seven nights a week."

"Is it the same every—"

"Of course not, silly."

"Ah . . . How often do you watch it, Clemmie?"

"Whenever I feel . . . oh, *you* know!" She giggled. "I watched it a lot while you were gone on the Mars-shot."

My trouble was, once the shock value had passed, I couldn't get caught up in the Hour of Release. I could be disgusted, or nauseated, but rationally I knew it was just actors and bladders of chicken blood and special effects, and there was no dramatic illusion to carry me beyond that knowledge to emotional involvement. For one thing, nobody ever defended himself. For another, no plots, just unvarying awful destruction: blood and death and torture. Screams, groans, shrieks.

The illusion was even less compelling when I started to

recognize actors. I hadn't again caught the big-eyed fox who'd "died" that first night, but the knife-wielder of that show was finally written into a script as a victim. He and three others had just started torturing a woman in lace scanties when she stepped out of her bonds and pointed at him.

"Take him!" she commanded the others.

"No!" he said. He was holding out his hands in sudden supplication, backing away from the camera. "You must not! I am one of you! I—"

"Random selection," intoned the girl.

"The computer never lies," said one of the other baddies.

They crushed his thighs under a truck wheel. While he was screaming, they castrated him.

"Doesn't anyone *ever* object to these things?"

Clemmie was wiping her eyes after a nice cathartic cry while the cat bled to death. "Who . . . who could . . . object? It makes you feel so . . . cleansed."

At the Space Center, I'd been able casually to get a look at the Mission Blueprint for the flight *this* earth's Zeke Dooley had gone out on. Same day, hour, second as my flight from *my* earth. Same crew, Long and Jackson and Dooley. So who would ever believe I was from an alternate universe? Not even Clemmie, the only one I'd tried my theory out on.

So here I was, and never going to get back, so why not lean back and enjoy it? Accept *this* Clemmie as *my* Clemmie, learn to swallow the Hour of Release as a cathartic, and try to overlook the differences from my own universe.

Right on, man. But when I got home from work that night, just as dusk was switching the streetlights on, a young dude in mod clothes ran into me on the sidewalk in front of the house.

"We know," he said quickly, helping me up. "We will try to contact you again when your . . . grief has subsided. Remember my face."

Then he was gone, down the sidewalk with a rather swishy walk that was very distinctive from the rear. I went up the front walk with my head in a whirl. *We know. Who* knew? What did they know? That I was from another universe? *When your grief has subsided.* What grief?

"How's your wife, Mr. Dooley?"

It was old man Jennings, out in his yard looking over his roses for aphids.

"Fine, I guess. Why?"

"The ambulance took her away about four o'clock. I thought . . . I'd hoped . . ." He had a stiff embarrassed look on his face. "I'm sorry. I'm truly sorry . . ."

It was like getting socked in the gut, entering the empty house. What could have happened? A fall? A sudden illness? Then who had called for help? Why hadn't I been notified at the Space Center? I went over and banged on Jennings' door, but he'd either gone out or wouldn't answer it.

Emergency services, that was it. Police rescue units. Private ambulance companies. Hospitals.

No police. No private ambulances. Neither one existed in this society. But there were hospitals, government ambulance dispatch centers, fire department emergency units.

An hour later I had nothing. Nobody had dispatched any ambulance to our address. Nobody had admitted a patient with Clemmie's name. Describing her when I got down to calling about unidentified accident victims didn't do any good, either. Young black women since four o'clock, sir? There aren't any black women, sir. There aren't any blacks.

Of course there *were*, but everyone in this idiot society had been so conditioned to believe that everybody was the same that they couldn't see the difference. Differences of race, for everyone but me, had ceased to exist.

I started in on the neighbors, ringing doorbells. Did you see an ambulance pull up at the Dooley house? *That* house. Right over there. You did? Did the ambulance have a name, a number, any . . .

Nothing to identify it at all. But everyone very sympathetic, almost solicitous. "I'm sorry. I'm truly sorry . . ."

As if they'd done it themselves.

The swishy young man returned to my mind. *We know. We will try to contact you again when your grief has subsided. Remember my face . . .*

Clemmie must have been *really* sick, taken bad. Something highly contagious, maybe, so they'd had to isolate her? Take her to a special medical facility that wasn't publicly listed?

That reminded me of my own medical isolation under the space program, so I called the duty officer to get Harginson's home phone.

—The general is unavailable, sir.

—This is an emergency, damn you.

—Sorry, sir.

But an hour later Harginson called me. "Duty officer's been through on the blower, Dooley," he barked. "Something about an emergency . . ."

I poured out the whole story for him. When I'd finished he was strangely silent. Then he gave a long sigh.

"Unmarked ambulance, interns without insignia on their hospital whites to show what institution they were from . . ." Another pause. "What damned rotten luck, man. After everything you've been through! But . . . well . . . We both

149

know it's just random, don't we? And . . . well . . . I can only say I'm sorry, Dooley. Truly sorry . . ."

I killed a bottle and slept on the couch.

I was brushing my teeth and wondering if four aspirin would help my head, and wondering what in God's name I could do to find Clemmie, when the doorbell rang. He was an early thirties type with crisp wavy hair cut almost painfully tight to his skull and sideburns that damned near cleared the tops of his ears. The eyes of a shark.

"Mr. Dooley? I'm Doctor Mauvais—"

I was dragging him in by the arm. "How is she, doc? *Where* is she? What's the matter? What happened—"

"I don't have anything to do with that." He gently disengaged his arm and led me into my own living room. "I know how you feel, I really do. Believe me, it's my job to understand what tension and pressure can do to a man. But you must understand that in this case there's nothing I can do. Nothing *anyone* can do. As you know, the computer never lies."

I could have squeezed the bastard's neck until his eyes popped out—*wanted* to, in fact—but he was the first person I'd talked to who would even admit knowing that Clemmie existed.

"When can I see her?" I said.

He gave me an odd look; then a speculative, almost feverish look came into his eyes. He said almost lasciviously, "Tonight." Then he was suddenly all business. "But right now, we want to know about the disturbed individual who contacted you last night. Young, slender person, with a slightly feminine way of walking. We would like very much to know what he said to you."

Who the hell was *we?* But I didn't ask. I didn't want to

antagonize him; he knew something about Clemmie. Even so, I was careful to make my voice thoughtful, and screwed up my face as if in remembering. This cat Mauvais was starting to smell like pig to me, whatever he called himself.

"Ah . . . He said something like, 'We know. We'll . . . ah . . . get in touch with you after your grief is over.' Something like that."

Mauvais was leaning forward with an intense look on his face.

"Are you *sure* that's all he said?"

I put on my act again. "Oh. Yeah. He told me to remember what he looked like."

"As if you would be seeing him again?"

"Something like that."

He stood up, all smiles, looking very satisfied as if he had confirmed something. He told me I'd been very cooperative and started for the door. When he was there, I called to him.

"Doc, about my wife—"

"It will be tonight, Mr. Dooley." Again that simper on the face. "Enjoy yourself."

It was the longest day I've lived. What do you do, man? Clemmie . . . *somewhere*. Sick with . . . *something*. Supposed to see her tonight . . . *sometime*.

They'd probably come and take me to her, I decided. Probably after six o'clock—Mauvais had said *tonight*. I wanted to call Harginson to find out if he knew anything about Doctor Mauvais, but was afraid to tie up the phone that long in case they tried to reach me with the news where I might see my wife.

Sure, okay, my almost-wife on this almost-earth, but I was beyond that sort of distinction with Clemmie now. She was *my* Clemmie.

151

Six o'clock. Nothing. By seven I'd been on the front porch twice to ring my own bell, making sure it was working. By eight, I'd started calling the weather bureau, just to hear the first words of the taped message and hang up. It confirmed that the phone was working. By nine, I'd had my topcoat on and off a dozen times.

Ten-thirty. Those rotten bastards weren't going to call. I was walking around the living room actually wringing my hands. I stopped dead. What if she was . . . What if . . . if Mauvais was on his way right now to tell me she'd died, his young earnest face long with lightly-felt sorrow? What if . . .

I made myself switch on the TV, sit down on the couch, crouched forward on the front edge of the cushion. I had to get hold of myself. Lights and colors blared. Shit. Eleven-twenty, right in the middle of The Hour of Release. Just what I needed right then.

It was a trial scene, ending hurriedly so they could get down to the chemical blood. The camera looked past the black defendant up at the three judges behind their massive polished desk. They wore powdered wigs and red satin-lined capes and were pulling on domino masks. Their movements were stylized, so they had the cadenced formality of ritual.

"YOU ARE GUILTY!" The one in the middle had a fine rolling voice to which I listened despite myself. "THE SENTENCE IS DEATH." The voice got almost arch. "BY WHATEVER MEANS THE EXECUTIONERS CAN DEVISE."

I went to the front door, opened it on a street lying quiet and serene under the lamps. Where in God's name *were* they? If nobody had come by midnight, I'd start tearing things apart to get hold of that nasty little bastard Mauvais.

On TV, the scene had shifted to a medieval-style dungeon. Black-clad torturers fluttered around the condemned fox like evil moths, stripping her and fondling her crudely exposed private parts. Taken with available light in long shot, the scene had a formalized nightmare quality like Doré etchings of Dante's hell.

I ran my little weather-check on the phone. Still live. I tested the front bell. Still live.

They had fastened the nude victim to the rack. The camera moved in to caress her body from breasts to knees as she was strapped down. One of the torturers, nude under his robe, began enjoying her sexually. It aroused me, sending me to the front porch sick and shaken at my own reaction. With Clemmie missing, sick in God-knows-what institution . . .

Cool air swept over me, laden with the delicate fragrances of Jennings' roses. The bald-headed old bastard probably was glued to the Hour of Release like damned near everyone else on the block.

As if on cue, behind me sudden harsh shrieks of agony started. They drew me back to the living room. I could almost smell the burned flesh as the branding iron bit into her flat smooth belly. She yelled again, her body jerking and writhing as if from an electrical charge.

The man who'd sexually pleasured himself upon her now was bending over her breasts, seizing one in his left hand. He held a knife in his right hand. His body hid the hand as it began making sawing motions. Her screams filled my ears. The man with the poker had gotten another glowing red.

The camera panned across him as he lunged forward with it between her spraddled legs, across the second man as he came erect waving something bloody aloft in his left hand, to zoom in on her dying face. Her mouth was strained impossibly wide, emitting an unformed animal sound of agony. My own mouth gaped with hers, my own formless screams echoed hers. Bloody froth bubbled up from between her gaping jaws. I fell forward to my knees on the rug. I began gently beating the floor with my fists. Someone had the conscience to be crying uncontrollably. I felt the tears on my face.

Mauvais. *Tonight you can see your wife. Enjoy yourself.* Knowing, he had assumed that I knew also, and wanted to watch Clemmie die.

Without moving my face, I was sick on the rug.

Hatred is a clean emotion, it burns as bright as thermite. Especially when it is mixed with a terror almost atavistic. But how do you get at them when a whole world has deluded itself into thinking that man is only a shaped charge fashioned by environment, and is never responsible if the nitro is joggled too hard and explodes?

A whole world knowing that nightly it witnesses real deaths, real agonies, real tortures, real perversions of mind and spirit. And approving, under the delusion that man cannot choose evil. Only Zeke Dooley, interstellar interloper farted by his universe through a black hole, had been in ignorance. Only Zeke Dooley had disapproved.

But wait a minute. *We will try to contact you again when your grief has subsided. Remember my face.*

The words took on new meaning. He had known Clemmie had been taken. Had been seeking to recruit me into . . . what? Some underground opposition which recoiled from the stench of roasting flesh and the howls of the victims? I could only wait until I saw him again.

I saw him the night after Clemmie's death. I saw him die on The Hour of Release. I had tuned in because that broadcast was the enemy, naked and exposed. His hypocrisies, his thought processes, the guts of what made him work. So I was watching when my only contact with the underground died. Horribly. I remembered his face, all right, even though he had no eyes left to see the ruin his body had become before he finally expired.

I knew despair. How had they found him? From what I had told them? But Mauvais had acted as if he already knew what we had said in the brief exchange. But that would mean "Doctor" Mauvais was really . . . Sure, of course, someone in security police under a more palatable disguise. As medical men, those supposed to succor mankind. That was when the hatred took direction. Mauvais. And his masters.

So they'd already had the fruiter revolutionary under surveillance. Then why hadn't they picked him up before? And how had they known what we had said when . . .

Wait a minute. Maybe there was routine surveillance of *everyone*. Visual and audio sensors to monitor *everything*. That was it. I had only to look, with an engineer's eye, and I saw them everywhere: every lightpost carried its scanners, almost every light socket. Inside the houses and out. I wondered if the average citizen knew—or cared.

Somewhere there were men who *did* care. But how to reach them? How to communicate without being observed and ruthlessly destroyed? You're a computer engineer, Zeke baby. Be logical. *Analyse*. I dig it, daddy. First step: *identify* your potential allies. Second: figure out a way to contact them.

Step one was easy. Four days after Clemmie's death, I was standing before an anonymous desk in an anonymous government office. Behind the desk was Mauvais.

"You aren't going to be difficult, are you, Mr. Dooley,

because your wife was one of those chosen by the computer for The Hour of Release? I assure you I regret the fact deeply, but . . . it *is* a random selection which no man can change."

A random selection like the revolutionary who died a couple of nights ago? I put on my quizzical look. In the world I had come from, brother, spades learned early how to dissimulate.

"Difficult, Dr. Mauvais?"

"Blaming me or my department for your wife's unfortunate demise." He swung a languid hand at a file on his desk. "Nothing in your *dossier* suggests such emotional illness, but . . ."

Nothing in my *dossier,* baby, because I ain't in it. I ain't in *anybody's* personnel file in this horror of a world, baby. I leaned forward, sincerity gleaming in my eyes. Old Bojangles, dancin' for them nickels.

"Nothing like that, Dr. Mauvais. I want to join your department."

It shook him. It really did. He cleared his throat. "That is . . . an unusual request, Mr. Dooley. The first we've had from a survivor of one of the . . . selectees. Might I ask why?"

"I watched that night, when Clemmie got it," I said.

Avidity entered his face. "And?"

"I realized I'd enjoyed it."

It was there in his face. He was going to explore it. Triumph sang in my temples like hypertension. I was going to end up a security agent, because he was going to find me the most apt pupil he'd ever had.

Security. The people with the power, because they had the *files.* The files of those who opposed the state's designs. The people I needed to contact.

Once I knew *who,* I still had to think of *how.* How, when the state's electronic ears and eyes were everywhere listening, watching, probing? There might be a way. It would depend on getting in good with Mauvais first, convincing him I was as sick as he was. It would mean zestfully spiriting away and killing the innocent. But once I had access to those files, once I was on the *other* side of those scanners . . .

I might just have figured out the blind spot.

Exactly six months ago tonight, Clemmie died. Tonight the first test of the blind spot will take place. I am sitting beside Mauvais right now, in his office. Waiting. He doesn't know that, of course. He thinks I am here merely to sip his brandy and listen to his tales of torture. He is head of security, he is the one who chooses who will die while passing it off to his superiors as computer selection. He saw Clemmie on the street one day, and coveted her. His joy is in destroying whatever his aesthetic sense finds beautiful. And so she died.

Oh, yes, we have talked about it. Often. I have become much more than underling and apt pupil. I have become a friend. I would like to sink my teeth into his jugular. He is describing his reactions when he dressed up as a torturer (complete with domino mask to disguise his features) so he could disembowel a twelve-year-old boy on television.

"When I plunged my hand into his intestines, I felt so much empathy that I dirtied my pants. Isn't that interesting?"

"Fascinating," I say. Practice has made me able to say it with no tinge of sarcasm, with utter sincerity. He sighs with contentment.

"You have a brilliant future with this department, Zeke."

"Thank you, Doctor."

My eye is on one of a dozen monitors banked across his

office wall. *The* monitor. The one on which the test will appear. Twelve men involved, all of them now dead. Three blacks, three yellows, three whites, three browns, hoarded carefully by me from the victims that *had* been computer-chosen. Doing what I told them for the camera, mistakenly believing it would save their lives.

It hadn't. My secret had died with them. I hope.

"Don't you ever regret leaving the Space Agency, Zeke?" he asked.

"Not for a single moment," I reply.

So many things unthinkable on this planet. Races, for one. No blacks or browns or yellows or whites here to anyone's eye but mine. Unthinkable. So I'd shot the little strip of film, developed it myself, trading outrageously on my favored status with Mauvais, the all-powerful Director of Health Services. Had fed the cartridge of film into the live coverage coming over this scanner. Seeing it, Mauvais would believe it was actually taking place on the rapid transit station platform that scanner covered.

"Why not?" he probes, wallowing in it. I look at him with limpid sincerity, thinking that his hide would make a wonderful lamp shade.

I begin, "Well . . ."

I pause. On the monitor, my film is starting. My twelve doomed players, acting as if their lives depend on their performance. Sorry, boys.

"Well, what?" he asks pleasantly, reaching for his brandy snifter.

"What's happening on monitor seven?" I ask.

Mauvais, soulless bastard, looks up sharply. I cast an eye toward him. He is staring, unbelieving. My actors have begun milling around at the door of one of the rapid transit units.

"They're fighting!" Mauvais exclaims. No one fights here. They've been conditioned out of belief in their aggressions.

Mauvais half-rises from his chair to contact security agents. I turn up the sound of monitor seven very loud, so we can hear the voices.

"Watch where you're going, nigger!"

"You goddam slant, who do you think—"

The epithets fill our ears. I look over at Mauvais. He is settling back, his placid, contemplative look returning.

"Kike!"

"Jig!"

"Honky!"

"Wop!"

Fists are thudding on faces. Mauvais is sniffing his brandy, swirling it in the cupped crystal to release its aroma most fully.

"You were saying you don't regret leaving the Space Agency—"

Freud, with his usual genius for misnomers, called it *negative hallucinations*. Another Viennese, Breuer, didn't do much better with *hysterical conversion*. Misleading, both terms. Nothing hallucinatory or hysterical about it. Moebius used *vacancy in consciousness*. Better. Better yet, *deliberate amnesia of defense*.

"Hebe!"

"Chink!"

Thud thud thud.

Today it's called *denial*.

Denial. A defense mechanism by which the conscious mind refuses to accept something the subconscious tells it is true. So the subconscious obligingly buries it. As if it had never happened. It was happening right in front of Mauvais, but he wasn't seeing it. For him it wasn't happening. While it was going on, anybody could say anything to anyone, could plan anything—and he wouldn't see it. *No* one would, not one of those over-conditioned security guards manning the scanners. Meets could be set up, actions planned, right in front of the scanners, as long as something this society had been conditioned to think was unthinkable occurred around the meet so the observers would go into a psychological state of denial

"Spade!"

"Dago!"

"Greaser!"

"Coolie!"

Everyone trained by the state to believe there are no races, cannot be any, cannot be any difference between men, either. No poverty, no prejudice, no aggression, no personal responsibility, no moral guilt.

So you cannot afford to admit it, even when you see it. You refuse to admit you saw it. It isn't there. You refuse to accept—*denial*—the situation, the fact, the sight, which upsets your preconceptions. Because to admit that situation or fact or sight would cause you grief, humiliate you, bring you extreme emotional pain.

"You were saying, Zeke?" repeats Mauvais courteously.

I swirl the brandy in my own snifter. Next week I will contact the underground. I already know them, their names, their haunts, their descriptions. And now I know *how* to go about it. Through the prejudices of this prejudice-free society we outlaws will destroy them all.

And among the first to go . . .

"I was going to say," I tell Mauvais, "that I can't conceive of enjoying anything more than I will these next months. . . ."

160

Among the first, Mauvais. He's dead, that motherfucker, he just doesn't know it yet. Doesn't know that the computer—now serviced by bad-ass Zeke Dooley—is going to randomly select Doctor Anton Mauvais as the subject of an evening's sport on The Hour of Release.

Stanley Ellin's novel Mirror, Mirror, on the Wall *blurred the distinction between mystery and mainstream. It showcased his specialty of putting the final factual and/or psychological revelation in virtually the last line of a story— or in this case, a novel. I tried to emulate him in this tale of a man on a deadly assignment who picks up a strange and beautiful and sexy woman—with results that surprise them both.*

YOU'RE PUTTING ME ON, AREN'T YOU?

I drove into the state capital at ten o'clock on Friday morning. I could have flown, but I had some potential clients in the two states *en route;* and personal contact, I felt, was the best way to announce that I'd taken over Dad's business since his death three months before. It was a big bustling city made with new money, mainly defense contracts, so I laid out extra bread for a motel on the Interstate beltline around town. One of those ultramodern plastic jobs with precast ceilings, glass tops on all surfaces, indoor-outdoor carpets to make shampooing up the spilled drinks easier, and color TV in every room.

After checking in, I went to meet the clients and to iron out the procedural details. The tension started building during the busy forenoon, increased during a numbing cafeteria luncheon, was like piano wire by 2:30, when all the equipment had been tested. I was due back at 6:30, and my outlying motel would spare me the evening rush hour during my return.

Back at the motel I did a few lengths of the pool, then laid on the sun-warmed cement to work on my tan and to relax. I was still Dad's untested replacement; *I* knew I was professionally competent, but the clients didn't. Not yet. Because I was turning it around in my mind, I didn't tune in the blond at first. Then, suddenly, I did. Her wet bikini just emphasized what it covered—as it was designed to do—and the late-slanting sun caught the rounded swell of her breasts and buried provocative shadows between them. I had to deliberately switch off. Work to do.

But then she came over and sat down on the cement beside me. Up close she was even better. I dug her looks, her build, the lazy challenge in her smoky gray eyes.

"This place is a drag, man. You groove?" She was assessing my body as she spoke with an impudent half-smile on her face.

"Then why stay here, baby?"

She ran a delicate pink tongue over full lips. "Study the animals. All the nowhere people, y'know? I mean, all you cats who always just got a haircut yesterday." Then, without any break at all, she said, "Want to buy me supper tonight, Mr. Straight?"

"Sorry," I said, and meant it. "I'm just here for one day from out of state, and I have to be to work in two hours."

She stood up with a sinuous grace. "What kind of work can you do at night? Lizbeth Hunter, room two-oh-two. I'll wait until nine o'clock before I go eat."

I stared regretfully after her, watching the enticing play of her taut backside under its whisp of bikini. Dammit. No matter how good-looking or well-built you are, prime stuff like that is always hard to get. And I had to work! And the job was damned important, too, since it was my first for this client. A real bummer all around.

But the job was a breeze. At 8:35 p.m. I was all finished and exactly six hundred dollars richer. And wound up tighter than a spring, crackling with tension like electricity. Well, still time to call her. A tall rangy cat named DeVille was standing around in his rather threadbare midnight-blue suit, so I asked him for a phone. He let me into an empty office.

"We'll make it the best place in town—your choice," I told Lizbeth when she answered the phone. "Twenty minutes. Be ready."

"Can I drive that groovy Porsche of yours, Mr. Straight?"

"We're vibing together, Miss Hip," I told her, and hung up.

DeVille walked down to the parking lot with me, the overhead sodium lights catching the strong planes of his jaw. He was a big man with a hard taciturn face and thick blond hair graying rapidly. Guys like him turn me off; they should know better than to think in stereotypes.

"You're younger than I expected."

"I've been voting for five years." Then I added, "Age isn't relevant anyway. Once you understand the physics involved, and know the mass you're dealing with, it's all mechanical."

He rested blunt fingertips on the hand-rubbed fender of my six-cylinder Porsche, twelve coats for a sheen deep enough to dive into.

"All just a matter of mass and physics, huh?"

"That's it."

I opened the door and he jerked back as if the fender had burned him. He hadn't realized it was my car. Stereotypes again. I rolled down the window to grin at him.

"Got to split, DeVille. I've got a heavy date with a blonde."

Lizbeth's choice of restaurants was French and surprisingly good. I had *rognons bourguignonne en croûte*—I'm very partial to innards, well-prepared—and she, at my suggestion, had a *noisette d'agneau Montpensier* so we could share a superb Romanee Conti '59. Her red mini was cut low enough to assure me that she wore no brassiere; that, and the look in those smoky gray eyes, made me feel that the expensive wine wouldn't be wasted.

But it nearly was, at that, and for the same reason that she appealed to me in the first place—because she was such a swinging, wiggy sort of chick. Being that, she felt she had to put everything down. The Establishment, the suburbs, the pigs, Vietnam, people who could afford twenty-dollar-a-day motel rooms without big monthly allowances from their parents. She'd told me about that over brandy.

"Are you trying to put *me* down too, baby?" I asked lightly.

I thought she'd say I was a swinger, but instead the gray eyes were cool and appraising. "Maybe I will at that, Mr. Straight."

Which secretly bugged me, because I pride myself on being with it. And then, while we were waiting for the car, she did it again.

"Going to fink out about letting me drive the Porsche, dad?"

I *didn't* want her driving it, actually; but the direct challenge gave me a tremendous urge to put *her* down. Hard. To crack the veneer.

"Why should I, baby? It's insured."

She gave a joyous laugh. "*Insured?* Beautiful! Hold that thought, man."

The battle lines were drawn. Once behind the wheel she gave me an appraising glance, then floored it. The Porsche wound up and howled. One-twenty. One-thirty. One-forty.

Oh, it was a groove, man. Doing her own thing, wild and free, like the student anarchist putting everyone down by planting his bomb in a school locker. Then it explodes prematurely and blows his hands off, and he suddenly discovers what a drag it is to type term papers with his elbows.

My hands were clenched and sweat dotted my upper lip by the time we reached the motel, but I had maintained external cool. That one was a draw. In my room she bounced down on the bed letting her legs sprawl carelessly open to show a tempting length of inner thigh and a whisp of black lace. I was in. She was accepting my terms. The bed would be the battleground. But first, she rummaged in her handbag.

"A contribution to the evening's festivities," she said.

I opened the twist of foil, knowing what to expect. Pot. The twice I'd tried it, maryjane hadn't shown me a thing beyond a mild disorientation, mainly spatial. Acute constipation or high blood pressure can do the same thing.

Her voice was challenging. "Will Mr. Straight smoke grass?"

What the hell, I thought, give her one. She had accepted my battleground. "Nope. Getting busted is bad for business, baby."

She laughed in triumph, stood up, and stripped off the dress in one quick, suddenly impatient movement. Her body was terrific. "Leave on the lights," she said. "I like to watch in the mirror."

It should have been easy: merely find a sex kick she didn't dig. Most of these ultrahip chicks, made safe by the pill, will go down for any stud who turns them on; but they're actually about as far out sexually as grandma was. But Lizbeth was different. She had a genius for corruption.

The bed was where it was at for her, and by dawn we'd done everything I'd ever done or thought of doing or *dreamed* of doing with a chick. And yet neither of us had come up with anything so degrading that the other refused, so neither had been able to put the other down.

At seven-thirty she rolled off me for a final time, lit a cigarette, and stuck it between my swollen lips. In reflex action I slapped it away, then realized my tactical error even as my hand moved. She squealed like a little girl, quick to press her advantage.

"Ohhh! Is ums poor mans afraid of ums big bad cancer bugs?"

The bitch. "I just don't like the goddamn things."

I couldn't admit that I *was* afraid of cancer, deathly afraid, since my Dad's death; couldn't admit that I woke up sweating at night in terror of not having quit in time, of having the goddam mushroom cells already ambushed and waiting in my body.

But that cigarette triggered in my mind a way to put her down. The smouldering black patch growing on the rug had become another contest between us; neither would admit to being concerned enough to put it out. Then, watching the fibres die, I suddenly got it.

These way-out types, they dig life without understanding where its true meaning really is at. As a result, they all want to stop war, stop pollution, stop hunting, save the little flowers by the roadside. So if I could put her on about myself, lead her on by circuitous logic to believe Mr. Straight, it would be a terrible put-down for her.

I got a glass of water, dumped it on the rug, and got back into bed—all with an abstracted, busy air that made her hostile and watchful. I'd given up too easily, you see.

And then I said, "I've been thinking, baby. About us."

"Us?" Her eyes flashed. She'd caught me being uncool. "You mean like a close personal relationship? Like *love?* Man, that's just another ego trip."

For one minute, I didn't answer. Try it some time. Sixty seconds is a long time in a conversation if no one converses. Finally I stirred myself to look over at her.

"Who said anything about love?"

"Well, like, ah . . . all you straight cats think . . ."

"How do you know I'm a straight cat? All I said was that getting busted is bad for business."

She shrugged it off scornfully. "Another straight hypocrisy; trying to make your money-grubbing sound groovy." She paused for a moment. "Next you'll claim you're like outside the law or something. . . ."

Beautiful. Doing my work for me, forestalling the suggestion, putting herself on. Beautiful.

"I'm not claiming anything, baby," I said carelessly.

Silence again while our meeting yesterday churned around in her head. *I'm just here for one day from out of state, and I have to be to work in two hours.* And her: *what kind of work can you do at night?*

Finally, unwillingly, she said, "So, like, what is it?"

She was hooked. She'd hooked herself. After waiting a second as if undecided, I hitched myself up on an elbow to grin at her.

"Let's call this a fable, Lizbeth. Let's suppose there are a bunch of cats who don't dig another cat because of something he's done. Something like—well, maybe he's tapped one of them out, dig?"

"No," she said flatly. But her eyes were searching my face intently now, seeming to find something there which disturbed her.

"So a dozen of them or so get together and decide they

have to get rid of this other cat. Just . . . take him out. Cancel him. But of course it might be dangerous or . . . unseemly to do it themselves, dig?"

"No," she said again. But softly this time, softly, her smoky gray eyes fixed on me with something almost frightened moving in them.

"So they naturally look around for another cat who can do the job for them. A cat from out of state, say—not from their own area at all. A specialist, dig? A sort of . . . *professional* man."

I played for effect on the last two words, and she said again, "No." Her voice was still soft, but it had a sort of entreaty in it by then. "No, no, no . . ."

"It's done all the time," I assured her, purposely obtuse.

"No, please, you . . . you're putting me on—aren't you?"

It was a gas. She was trying to deny to herself that I could be a hit-man. That her carefully seductive supper and incredible sexual coupling afterwards had been with a . . .

"You're . . . you've *got* to be putting me on. You wouldn't . . ."

But of course I *would,* her brain told her. That's just what a pro *would* do. He'd want to pump out all the sexual arousal engendered by tapping someone out. Hell, she would have read all about it in her text books, she would have majored in psych or soc or lit. They all do.

"Come *on,* baby!" Time for the overkill. I used the hearty, coaxing voice that guys wearing convention buttons use on chicks they meet in hotel bars. "It's just a story! A fable, like Faulkner won the Nobel prize with." I stood up, very cool, very casual. "Look, I'll catch a quick shower, a shave, then we'll eat breakfast and split."

I was into the bathroom with the door shut before she could react. Under a hard hot shower I let out the laughter in huge whoops. Talk about a *put-on!* She'd be out there right now, trying to tell herself she *couldn't* have spent the night balling with a killer. But if she hadn't . . . why, if she hadn't, then she'd just been terribly put on by Mr. Straight himself.

And she wouldn't be able to take that, either. When I went back into the room she would be gone; and the delicious part would be that she'd never know, for sure, one way or the other.

But she fooled me: when I came out of the bathroom, I saw the six one-hundred dollar bills I'd been paid with the night before. All laid out on the bed. And she still was there, too, in her red mini once more, pressed back against the wall beside the door.

"That money was in your wallet!" she cried accusingly.

Of course. Her sort of wiggy chick had too big an ego factor not to *know* if she'd been put on. So she'd snooped for proof—and had found it. To her, those bills would be "hit" money from the "syndicate" or whoever she thought had hired me.

Man, it was beautiful. But before I could laugh, a heavy fist pounded on the door.

"Open up in there! This is the police!"

"I called them," she cried triumphantly. "While you were in—"

The door burst open and a big man in a rather threadbare midnight blue suit came through smoothly, his .38 Policeman's Special arcing the room for quarry. I froze, feeling damned silly because my towel might fall off any second. Oh, sure, for Lizbeth it was the ultimate, literal cop-out: she'd run screaming to the hated pigs. But at the moment I couldn't savor my victory. The fuzz I could do without.

At least it was one I'd met. DeVille sighed and rammed

the snub-nosed revolver back into his belt holster.

"You *told* me you had a date with a blonde." he said. "But where did she get the idea you were a Mafia hit-man?"

Before I could answer, Lizbeth cried, "Why are you putting your gun away? He's a hired killer! He . . . he *bragged* about it! He . . ."

"Bragged?" DeVille's cop-hard eyes raked me briefly with a sort of sick speculation, then swung back to her. "Bragged about what?"

So she went ahead and told it, the whole fable about the hired outsider and all the rest. It should have been pretty humorous to someone with the facts, so I kept waiting for the laughter to boil up out of DeVille when he realized that she had taken me for a hired killer. But no laughter came. Instead, he started to look as if he were chewing on a mouthful of maggots.

"Dammit, DeVille, it was just a put-on," I burst out finally. A drop of sweat was trickling down my bare spine; this clown, after all, could affect my professional future. "A put-on, get it? A joke. I was just having a little fun with her."

"Fun?" His eyes moved from her, to me, to the sweat-soaked bed, as if able to see us working grimly and lovelessly away there on each other. "What gets me is the dozen guys who got together and hired another guy to . . . *Fun?* Jesus!"

He turned away but Lizbeth, still not understanding any of it, seized his arm almost hysterically.

"You can't just leave!" she cried, her face distorted. "He said . . . he talked about killing someone last night! He—"

"He did kill someone last night," said DeVille bluntly. "He executed him. He's a professional hangman."

I find that when I write about the future, the stories emerge as angry—or at least quite devoid of hope. So I tried to lighten things up with "The Andrech Samples" while being true to my feeling that mankind is breeding itself and our planet into oblivion. Hence our tale: in a future society a man and wife must do terrible things to save their unborn infant. . . .

THE ANDRECH SAMPLES

Riding the personnel transport belt up to the level of Rogul's office, I wiped my hands down my thighs. I never had killed anyone before. Never had wanted to. Hell, I didn't want to now. But since yesterday it had been sure. I wiped my hands again. Clammy, even though I had seen no one since entering the building. They all had gone, all had crowded to the heli-ports, all had been fed by aerial arteries into the residence blocks for the usual evening tele.

All except Rogul.

I stopped outside his office, wiped my palms nervously again; then I stepped forward to break the light beam. The tele-screen above glowed with the color image of Rogul, made familiar by two months of patient stalking and watching.

"Mr. Andrech?"

"That's right." I was amazed at the steadiness of my voice. "I hope I'm not too late . . ."

"Oh, no, no. I had a lot of work to catch up on. Come in please."

I broke the second light beam and went through the

172

opening door to his inner office. First time I'd been there, of course; wouldn't do to have his secretarial robot able to identify me later.

Rogul was behind his desk, standing: a tall, gray-haired, well-conditioned man in his late forties. A self made man who had come up a dozen years before with a new design for mass transport of planetary settlers which had made him wealthy. We shook hands.

"So, Andrech. You claim to have developed cheap artificial atmospheres for small, low-gravity planets. Is that true?"

"I have."

I'd needed a cover story, in case his secretary still had been switched on, or a business associate still had been present. But we were alone. I seemed to see each second stretch out long and thin around us, thinner and thinner, until finally it snapped and fell away.

"I hope so, Andrech. Even if there is overlapping between your design and the encased bubble atmosphere, a workable new process would be worth a great deal of money."

I went past him toward some abstract figurines on the window sill; I wanted him on his feet—with his back to me. I wasn't sure I could do it if he were sitting, and I didn't want to watch his face as the blade went in.

"These statues are . . . damned interesting."

"Unique, aren't they? The indigenous humanoids of Akaniam used to make them before . . ." His voice trailed off absently as he moved over beside me. "Seems a damned shame, actually."

I picked up a figurine, and then set it down again. "Before what?"

"Before they were exterminated. We had to, of course; Akaniam's close in, easy access." His eyes momentarily were sad: large, intelligent eyes, with whites so clear they had a bluish tinge. "We needed the land for settlers. We always do."

He turned from the window. Turned away from me.

Reflexes took over. My right arm flicked, the sleeve-knife slid its thin, razor-edged length from the plastic sheath strapped to my forearm. The same flow of movement swept the blade forward and into his kidney.

Rogul gave a hoarse cry of agony, his body arching back as it tried to contain the searing pain. My cupped left hand went over his shoulder to jerk his chin up and to the left as the knife pulled wetly free, slashing, then darted up in a lethal arc at his throat.

Bright arterial blood splashed across my fingers and jacket sleeve, making me jerk back as if it were scalding. The flaccid corpse collapsed on the tiles. It didn't even twitch. Rogul was dead.

I leaned against a corner of the desk, panting, sweat searing my eyes and dripping on the polished plastic so my fingers dragged wet smeary marks across the surface. I had done it, just as Delia and I had rehearsed a thousand times in the months since making our decision.

After slumping there for an eternity of those elastic seconds, head down, breath whistling raggedly through my clenched teeth, I straightened up with something like a sob. Averting my gaze from the pathetic huddle of cloth and flesh which had been Rogul, I went to his private sink and washed my hands. I didn't want to waste it all by drawing attention on the nearly deserted, post-rush helitrans home.

Delia knew the moment she saw me, with that instant rapport of people deeply in love; but she could say nothing because of the twelve other tenants with whom by regulation we shared a dwelling area. When we finally were in a bed cubicle with the beam switched on for privacy, she sank down slowly beside me on the edge of the bed.

"Poor darling. What have we done to each other? Killing . . ." Under the light synthetics of her pajamas, I could see the almost childish wings of her shoulder blades. She turned great tear-stained eyes at me. "Maybe we should just . . . stop—"

I stilled her words with my lips. This was the moment to be strong, I knew. I could feel her body heat through the pajamas. Her stomach still was flat but in that body, right now, was our child, embryonic yet, little more than a tiny heart pulsing in its warm dark bath of amniotic fluid, but *ours*. Yesterday's tests had confirmed it.

"We've been over all this, Delia. We're going through with it."

She drew a deep, shuddering breath. "So Mrs. Rogul too . . ."

"Not until tomorrow," I whispered against her fragrant hair.

We spent the time afterwards, until lights-out, giggling over our attempts to find mutually acceptable names for the baby.

Neither Delia nor I were psychologically prepared for waiting: time to study, to plan, to foresee, also meant time to remember the hot sticky gush of life's blood across my wrist, the broken cry of Rogul's anguish. And waiting might give Mrs. Rogul time to begin wondering whether it had been more than a random killing. So I went after her the next night, almost blindly. As it turned out, my direct approach made it ridiculously simple.

Amelia Rogul was childless, of course, a few years younger than her husband had been. A modern woman who loved life, used it, spent it, and thus who needed no friends beside her for support in grief. This meant she was alone, since the Roguls, as wealthy people, had a separate dwelling unit, even the luxury of separate cooking facilities.

I broke the entryway light beam and waited, an idiotic look of sorrow on my face, a blank tape deck prominent in my hand. I felt no compunction. Perhaps I had been brutalized by the first killing; perhaps, instead, it just was knowing that success was one body nearer.

"What is it, please?"

She hadn't illuminated, so I couldn't see her in the tele-screen as she studied me; but no nerves trilled in her voice. Good.

"I have a message of condolence from your husband's employees, Mrs. Rogul." Then, in a stroke of genius, I added, "If you want me to leave it here in the hall—"

That made her break the inner beam, of course, and step to the door to reach for the tape. "No need of that. I'll take it and—"

My hands came up to close about her throat. She made a sound like that of the great sea birds on tele'd historicals. The door had shut behind me; with the tele-screen blanked one-way, nobody passing in the hall could see us at all.

Even then I almost lost her. She brought a knee up, hard, just missing my manhood; I squinted and clawed my hands deeper into her throat. We went about it in an odd, clumsy, ritual dance. Her breath hissed in my face. Her hands flapped ineffectually against my steeled forearms, desperate fingers peeled skin from my forehead and shredded my jacket pocket. My own fingers were slimy with our mingled sweats.

Finally the movements lost volition. She became too heavy to support. My hands let the inert body slide to the floor, then felt for a pulse at the base of her throat. None. Spittle-flecked lips drawn back in a canine snarl, and I was surprised by a moment of acute nausea: her eyes protruded far enough to be knocked off with a sweep of a hand.

The sickness passed. I checked the hall through the tele-screen, then went home to give Delia the news.

Once again, sweaty palms. Personnel transport belt again, but this time to the Investigation Section, Metro Police. Waiting in the interrogation cubicle with nerves screaming. For Delia, it had to go right. For us both.

"Mr. Andrech?" The voice jerked my thoughts back. "I'm Inspector Ngaio. No, that's all right, please remain seated."

He was a big, solid man with probing eyes and a square chin. My voice came out almost falsetto. "I . . ." I stopped to clear my throat. "I came about . . . the Roguls."

"Right," he said easily. His manner was relaxed, and I felt my tensions ease a bit. "I have gone over the facts of your statement."

He stopped there. Sweat started up under my arms, the seconds began stretching as they had before I'd put the blade in Rogul's back.

Finally I blurted, "Inspector, the fingerprints alone—"

"—could have been made at an earlier date. None in the blood, remember, Andrech; just on the figurine and on the desk top."

"His secretarial robot will confirm that I was never there before . . ."

"You thought of that, did you?" Ngaio had a deep voice and deep masculine laugh. He was a good interrogator. "You're right, of course. Your photo elicits no response from the secretary's memory banks, yet your name is on

Rogul's calendar. And your fingerprints are in his office. You were there that night, all right, after the robot had been closed down. But the killing could have occurred *after* your departure."

"What about his wife, strangled the next day? Surely—"

"Coincidence, perhaps. Or even you, trying to cash in on the husband's death." He leaned forward. "Where's the murder weapon?"

My months of practice paid off. A single fluid movement and the stiletto lay gleaming on my palm. Ngaio sat up abruptly with a look of genuine pleasure on his face, as I said, "I didn't clean the blade."

"I'll be damned. A *sleeve* knife. Haven't seen one in years." He held out his hand for the knife. "That was very good. And the blade uncleaned. I begin to believe you are a very determined man, Andrech."

His robot, which had been tuned to monitor the conversation, came in. He handed it the knife. "Lab."

"It isn't just me, Inspector," I said earnestly. Both Delia and I want this Certificate very much. We knew this method of meeting the quota would be difficult, perhaps self-destructive, but we—"

"Why didn't you just buy a pair of emigrations? With new planets opening up all the time—"

"We can't afford to purchase someone's passage, Inspector. Not on the pay of a clerk in telemetry."

He switched the conversation abruptly. "How about blood from Rogul? Any get on anything except the knife?"

"The jacket sleeve. I wore the same one for Mrs. Rogul."

"Indeed? We found cloth fibers clutched in her hand . . ."

"The pocket. I took the liberty of leaving the garment with your laboratory on my way in. Also, since she scratched my forehead, I asked them to take blood samples."

"I'll be damned," he said again. He was impressed, I could see that; behind the detached official manner was a warm, genuine human being. He turned to punch into the laboratory. "The Andrech samples?"

"Positive," said the white-coated technician. "Victim's blood on knife and jacket sleeve; subject's blood and epidermis under second victim's fingernails; one-hundred percent match on the jacket fibers."

"Good. Thanks."

Ngaio blanked the screen and opened the folder on his desk. I felt the old clamminess start as he bent to write. What would a negative report do to Delia? But when Ngaio closed the file and stood up with two slips in his left hand, there was a wide grin on his face. My heart gave a leap of more than joy: of emotion too pure, too ethereal for mere words. He stuck out his right hand.

"Congratulations, Andrech. To you *and* your wife."

I felt I was beaming fatuously; it was all I could do to take his hand. "Thank . . . thank you, Inspector. For everything. I don't think we could have gone through it again."

"Now you won't have to." He handed me the slips. "The first is a regular *pro forma* misdemeanor citation, even though my investigation shows the killings were justified. You can pay the fine at the front desk on your way out. And this other one . . ."

I was beaming idiotically again. "Our Certificate."

"Right. Give it to your wife's gynecologist; it orders him not to abort her pregnancy as usual. Since you successfully have removed from the population rolls one couple, childless, you have met the quota requirements. As per law, you can have one child. And I hope it's a boy."

"So do I. Then we can name him after you, Inspector."

That pleased him; as I said, he was a genuinely decent human being. Then I was on the personnel transport belt again, descending to my waiting, beautifully pregnant Delia. As I watched the joy spring into her face at the sight of my own obvious elation, there was only one small cloud to darken the rosy glow on my mental horizon.

What if she were carrying twins?

During one bleak and icy Minneapolis winter, I was stuck with a job on a night loading dock because I needed the money. After work I'd go down the street to a local bar to thaw out. I got to know the regulars, and one night watched the real-life drama I use in this story play itself out. I always thought a crime news item I read in the newspaper the next day was the true and actual ending of the story—so I stole it for "Night Out."

NIGHT OUT

I wouldn't want you to think that I don't like men. It's just that I've known for a good ten years—ever since the hired hand on my daddy's farm followed me into the barn when I was twelve—that they're only interested in one thing. Knowing this has gotten me into the work that I do; but I won't even pretend that I don't get a tremendous thrill out of it each time, and a personal satisfaction that goes 'way beyond doing my job or earning my living.

Take last Sunday. I wasn't really looking for a night out; I'd just dropped into the *Lonesome Pine* for a beer after the movies. It's a narrow little bar between two pawn shops on Washington Avenue in the part of Minneapolis they call "skid row." As I raised my glass—they're only a dime and awfully big—this fellow laid a hand on my shoulder.

"How about a fresh beer, baby?"

He was a big man with a red face and he wore a storm coat and an expensive hat. But I was just there for a beer, so I said:

"No thank you, I don't drink with strangers."

"I'm no stranger, baby; I've seen you somewhere before." Men always get around to saying that so it never bothers me much.

"I'm sorry—one is always my limit."

Just then Joe came in the back door. He's nice but he's not very bright. Here it was nearly zero that night and all he had on was a pair of coveralls, and great big overshoes all buckled up, and a little white cloth apron that said *Master Lumber Co.* on it. He wore a workman's cap, too, with about twenty different out-of-date union buttons on it.

"Hey, Joe!" shouted Frank, who plays the drums in the band. "Did you bring your mouth organ with you tonight?"

"No—I'm too smart to bring my mouth organ to a place like this."

"Too smart, eh Joe?" Frank looked around and winked and a lot of people laughed. "I guess you are at that."

Joe shines shoes for a living. The wooden box he uses for a shine kit has a Kansas license plate nailed to it, a real one, and little miniature Minnesota and Wisconsin and Michigan license plates like used to come in Wheaties boxes. He started shining his flashlight on my legs, but I didn't mind; I've got nice legs and the man in the storm coat looking at them.

Joe said to me: "Frank asked did I bring my mouth organ along and I told him no, I was too smart to bring it to a place like this."

"I didn't know you had a mouth organ, Joe," I told him.

"Sure I do." He held out his hands about a foot apart. "A big one I got, two tiers. I play it all the time."

I never laugh at Joe like the others do; I understand him.

"I don't drink that damn stuff," he said all of a sudden. "It tastes like people wash their feet in it. I drink whiskey sometimes."

"On Sundays they only sell beer."

"Whadda ya mean? They sell Seven-Up."

He started blinking his light at the man in the storm coat, who growled like a bear and turned away. I could see that Joe bothered him, so before I even thought I said:

"He's not a very nice person, Joe. He made some insulting remarks to me just before you came in."

Joe walked right up to him and grabbed his arm.

"Whadda ya mean, talkin' to the lady that way? I shine shoes and pay my union dues; weren't for the union wouldn't get your gaddam shoes shined, whadda ya think of that?"

The man in the storm coat didn't say what he thought of that. He just jerked his arm loose and hit Joe right in the mouth. Joe fell down and his shine kit broke open and his flashlight went under the juke box. When he tried to get up, the man in the storm coat grabbed a bottle off the bar and hit him right on the side of the head with it, so the glass broke and cut Joe's face. Everybody stood up to see and someone screamed. The big man's eyes were all scared and wild, and I could feel the blood pounding in my temples.

Just then two cops came in; they always travel in pairs on Washington Avenue and are the biggest cops in Minneapolis.

"Okay, break it up." One of them had his club out and everything. "What happened here?"

"This crazy loon attacked me, so I poked him one. When he tried to get up he . . . knocked my bottle off the bar. I guess it broke and cut him."

"That the way it happened?" The cop with the billy club looked sharply around. After a minute Frank, who'd gotten off the bandstand, spoke up:

"That's right, officer. Joe there shines shoes around the

neighborhood. He's kind of a psycho, everyone knows that."

"You'll have to come down to the station house if you want to swear out a complaint, mister."

"Just get him out of here," said the man in the storm coat. He was sweating. "I don't want to bother with him; I don't want him near me."

"Your business, Jack." The cops took Joe's arms and hauled him off the floor. "C'mon, pal," said the second one, "We'll have the police surgeon take a look at that head."

After they were gone the man in the storm coat came over to me. He had a nice man-smell of shaving lotion.

"Baby, why'd you sic that screw-loose on me? I didn't mean to hurt him, but psychos give me the willies."

When he mopped his face with his handkerchief his hand was shaking, but his eyes still had the same look as before; I knew right then that I was going to have a night out after all. I made my eyes flash.

"You're a cruel man!" I exclaimed loudly, so people turned to look. "Hitting Joe with that bottle just because he stood up for me!"

Then I buttoned my coat around me and flounced out without looking back, so everyone saw me leave alone. In the street I turned left, toward the bridge, and walked slow. Sure enough, I'd gone only a block when I heard his heavy footsteps in the scrunchy snow behind me.

"Hey, look, baby, I wasn't being fresh back there."

"I knew you'd follow me."

He fell into step beside me. "You're a funny one. I thought you were sore 'cause I was such a brute."

I shook my head and giggled. "No you didn't, or you wouldn't have come looking for me."

"Hey, you're pretty sharp!" His eyes, going down to my

legs again, tried to undress me. "What's a sharp chick like you doing in that cheap dive?"

"Just a beer after the movies."

At the next intersection he took my elbow as if to keep me from slipping on the ice, and then put his arm around my waist. We turned down a side street and I leaned closer against him. He let his hand touch my breast. When we came to an alley alongside a grubby brick apartment building, I said:

"I live down there in the basement apartment."

"Alone?"

"All alone. When a girl has a roommate she can't do the things she wants."

We were in black shadow. There were three steps down and a niche in the wall that was just right. When I stopped he crowded up close against me. His voice was low and throaty.

"Are you going to invite me in, baby?"

I stood on tip-toe and kissed him, long and passionately like the movies. Then I drew back and rummaged in my purse as I always do, whispering: "I'll get the key."

He was tall and strong, and his face looked like the hired man's when I was twelve, just as I'd known it would, so I brought my right hand out of my purse and drove the ice-pick up into the bottom of his chin. My pick is filed down to five inches and I keep the point real sharp, so it goes in all the way to the wooden handle.

For a few seconds he just stood there swaying, a shocked look in his eyes; then he made that noise in his throat that they all make, and slid down the brick wall and tipped over sideways with his shoulder wedged against the door.

Looking down at him I felt awfully glad and all warm and sleepy inside, because he'd been another nasty man like the others. I pulled out my pick and wiped it on his shirt and put it back in my bag; then I went through his pockets and took the money from his wallet. He had a lot of money. I left him there and walked home.

I was talking with the waitress down at the corner today, and I think that this afternoon I'll buy a Greyhound ticket to Chicago. From what she told me, there are even more men in Chicago who try to pick up girls in bars than there are in Minneapolis; I ought to have some nights out that I'll never forget. I'll probably be able to start a savings account, too, because some of them are sure to be convention-goers with big expense accounts. I have to think about things like that; even though I'm working for the safety of all American women, I won't have any Social Security to fall back on when I'm ready to retire.

When Eleanor Sullivan was Editor-in-Chief of Ellery Queen's Mystery Magazine, she ran a series of covers featuring their regular authors in criminous contexts. My turn came when I was back east for the annual Mystery Writers of America banquet. After we finished the shoot on a left-over set in the photographer's downtown studio, I told Eleanor I wanted to write a story built around the cover photo. Thus this tale of a sweet, nerdy dreamer (with a sweet and timid wife) who finally gets his chance to be a private eye in a classic mould—or does he?

SLEEP THE BIG SLEEP

Murder.

My meat.

I'm Danny Durant. Two hundred forty-four pounds of bronzed dynamite, lightning in both fists, an Army Colt .45 automatic like Mike Hammer's under my arm (with seven notches in the walnut grip to remind me of the men I've killed), a bottle of Old Granddad in the desk drawer, a blonde hellcat in the bedroom.

Well, I guess that's not all quite true. The 244 pounds is really 144, and I look like Woody Allen in his stand-up-comedian days, right down to the heavy hornrims because I'm myopic (OD-1 sph/OS-1 sph) and contacts make my eyes tear up. Whoever heard of a tough P.I. looks like he's gonna bust out crying any second? Far from a blonde hellcat I have Emily in my bed, so small and dark-haired and intense she was nicknamed "Midge" in high school. And she's my wife besides.

I've gone this far, you may as well know the rest of it. I don't own a gun, I don't have a license to carry one, I've never *fired* one. I've never even punched anybody out—my mom wanted me to be a classical musician, so I couldn't do sports or anything for fear of damaging my hands. I took piano all through grade school and high school, then quit entirely as soon as I went away to college. Race Williams might play "The Minute Waltz" on some bozo's backbone, but on a *Steinway?*

But I do have my P.I. license. I worked for Dun & Bradstreet summers in college and several years full-time thereafter; no booze, blondes, or bullets writing D&B credit reports, but it gave me the hours of investigative field work to qualify for the P.I. exam. Which I creamed. I really studied for the legal parts of it, and as for the questions about procedure, Hammett's Op stories are a primer in the fine points of working those mean streets.

So I have my license and I have an office. Okay, so it's over our garage, but even Sam Spade had to start somewhere. My sign down at the end of the driveway has *We Never Sleep* arched over a big open eye like an eyebrow, and lettered underneath:

DANNY DURANT
Private Investigations
Cool—Careful—Confident—Discreet

I stole the eye from Pinkerton's and the adjectives from George Anson Phillips in *The High Window*—the only P.I. novel Emily ever read all the way through. George is a terrible detective, and gets killed besides, so his adjectives on my sign are the ironic gesture of the tough guy, full of bittersweet meaning. Emily just thought they were silly.

Our arguments, which have been getting more frequent, have always been about the same thing: my desire—no, my *need*—to be the uncaring, wise-cracking, unsentimental tough guy of the classic private-eye tale. Sam Spade. Philip Marlowe. Lew Archer. Spenser. Amos Walker. *Danny Durant!*

Emily has a point; of course; she's trying to get started as a psychotherapist just like I'm trying to get started as a private eye. But I have an office and she has to use an empty room at Public Health—she gets most of her referrals through her best friend Claire, who works there. Emily says it's like a lawyer taking *pro bono* work to get his name known.

Here I am hung up on the private-eye stuff, and Emily can't stand violence. Reason is, she's an orphan and she's had this recurring nightmare since she was five or six. This huge guy abducts her on a rainy, blowy, stormy night, takes her to a big sort of mansionlike place, and is going to do something terrible to her, but right at the last minute this sort of hero figure tries to rescue her. Either the hero dies, or the bad guy dies—she always wakes just before the end.

I'm not so sure it was just a nightmare. Maybe it's something that almost really did happen, that she's forgotten the way Anthony Galton did in *The Galton Case*—she doesn't know who her parents were. Maybe that's why she went into psychotherapy; trying to help herself by helping others. In the photo she has of herself at six, her eyes are dark and haunted.

So she really *hates* to be alone in a rainstorm at night. So of course we had this terrible argument on the night of this really grotesque cloudburst. Maybe the rain was to blame; I know it made my hair curl and my nerves jump and my skin itch just like the hot dry Santa Anas did in Chandler's *Red Wind*.

Anyway, Emily had tears in her eyes. "Danny, it has to stop! You just aren't cut out to be a hard-boiled private detective. If you were good at it that would be one thing, but we're broke and in debt and the house payment is coming up—"

"You don't know that."

"It's due the fifteenth of every—"

"You don't know that I'm not cut out to be a detective! Any more than we know you're cut out to be a psychotherapist."

"I have my Ph.D. I have my license in clinical psychology. I have clients. Some of them even pay me!"

"I've got my license, too."

"And how many clients in the six months since you put that crazy sign up?"

I said, with great dignity, "Just one. Billy Jenkins. But—"

"Who's twelve years old. Whose dog was missing."

"I found him, didn't I?"

"And got paid a dollar." Emily is a couple of inches shorter even than I am, with wavy brown hair and direct brown eyes and a slightly uptilted nose and lovely lips that even in the middle of the argument I wanted to kiss.

"Honey, I know it hasn't been easy," I said. "This isn't 'Frisco or LaLa Land or the Big Apple or even the Big Easy. Not even the Twin Cities. It's a little town in southeastern Minnesota where not much happens. I gotta get a rep, bust some bad guys, solve a big case—"

"Please, please, just *listen* to yourself, Danny! Whenever you go into that—that detective *lingo*—"

But then she melted into my arms. I didn't know if she was laughing or crying. Maybe a little bit of both. Her hair tickled my nose with a clean, herbal-shampoo smell.

"Oh, Danny, what are we going to do? You aren't the

tough, cynical, devious-minded man in those detective novels you read. You're sweet and gentle and bright and a dreamer, and those are the things I love you for. But you're ruining our lives with these fantasies! You know it's the split in you, your dark side coming out."

I said our arguments were about me wanting to be a tough private eye, but that isn't quite right. They were also about her telling me *why* I wanted to be a tough private eye.

It all went back, she always said, to the fact that a hunk of every man is defensive, angry, impelled by a non-rational urge for revenge against what it sees as the feminine. Because, according to Jung or Freud or somebody, when we're separated from our mothers we feel rejected and so we reject our own feminine side in turn, try to anchor ourselves in the masculine.

In men like me, sweet and gentle on the outside, our masculine ego gets isolated from the rest of the psyche and generates a shadow complex. This masculine dark side, repressed and what Emily calls ego-alien, rebels against patriarchal and paternal authority. Like Satan resisting God.

Get the picture? The sweeter a guy is, the more of a mess he is. And it gets worse. Because this savage sort of shadow figure gets together with that rejected feminine side and they form a psychological complex that gets projected onto real women. This complex sees women as evil, is scared of them.

And that, ladies and gentlemen, is why I want to be a tough private eye. And why Emily and I were always fighting. Because of my dark side. My repressed shadow figure. See what I mean? All of a sudden she was my therapist instead of my wife.

"Don't start that psychobabble again," I said. "I'm not one of your patients."

"Well, you ought to be."

Would Mike Hammer take that? Would Max Thursday? Heck, would Kinsey Millhone? V. I. Warshawski would kick a lung out of anyone said that to her. I grabbed my trenchcoat and fedora and paused in the open doorway to snarl the Op's speech to Princess Zhukovski in "The Gutting of Couffignal."

" 'You think I'm a man and you're a woman. That's wrong. I'm a manhunter and you're something that has been running in front of me. There's nothing human about it.' "

"Danny!" she cried behind me. "Don't go! Please!"

I shouldn't have, of course. Emily had gotten mad because she was scared. Of the night, of the dark, of the rain, of being alone. But I stopped only long enough to get the miniature airline bottle of whiskey out of my desk drawer, then I jumped into my old sedan and drove away from there.

As I followed the moving tunnel my headlights carved into the night, I felt at first like Lew Archer in the opening of "Gone Girl" as he tooled home from the Mexican border in a light-blue convertible and a dark-blue mood. But one trouble with stalking out of your own house in the middle of the night is that you don't have anyplace to go. After a while the wipers slapping their monotonous refrain against the windshield started to sound like *rotten guy, rotten guy.*

By then I was at the outskirts of Plummerton, a hundred miles from home. The town was named after Ezekiel Plummer. In the 1920s he had single-handedly brought the railroad through for the meat-packing plant that was still the town's chief industry. I was too exhausted to drive back in the rain, so I used the off-ramp to the access road, went by a couple of all-night fast-food restaurants, a shopping mall, and then spotted an old-fashioned flashing neon sign: VACANCY . . . VACANCY . . . VACANCY . . .

U-shaped place around a swimming pool whose dark surface was cratered by the rain's mortar fire. Cheery yellow light from the office. I splashed through the puddles to pay $19.95 plus tax—in advance because my only luggage was the airline whiskey miniature I'd brought from my desk drawer.

By then I was feeling pretty rotten about myself and Emily. I set the miniature on the bedside table and sat on the bed to call her. The phone rang. And rang and rang and rang.

I tried again. Emily wasn't home. Or if she *was* home—

I leaped up. I'd get back in the car and drive home right then, no matter how tired I was, no matter how—

No. She'd gone over to Claire's, that was all. When I'd been on the road for Dun & Brad, in lousy weather she'd always stayed over at Claire's. They'd been roommates and Claire was still her best friend and confidante.

After ten p.m. there was no answer at Claire's either. So they'd gone to a movie, stopped someplace for a snack after. I'd try again in a half hour.

I turned on the TV and lay down on the bed with my clothes on, water-spattered trenchcoat and all. I was Spenser in *Promised Land* and Susan Silverman had walked out on me because I wouldn't say I loved her. Spenser drank bourbon, I drank bourbon: a big slug out of the miniature. And coughed and choked. Wow! Whiskey all alone like that was really potent.

And the darn sound on the TV set didn't work. Too bad, because there was a private-eye thriller on, one of the old black-and-whites that colorization has made into antiques.

About this beautiful little dark-haired girl, only five or six, being kidnaped in the parking lot of a rainswept shopping mall.

I took a second, more cautious sip, emptied the bottle.

Even without sound, I can tell the passer-by who tries to stop the kidnaper is a wanna-be private eye who happens to be in the right place at the right time. What I wouldn't give for a chance like that! To face the bad guy, save the girl, show that I was like my heroes in the hard-boiled detective novels!

The kidnaper is a huge guy in black: black jeans, black Navy watch cap, muscles rippling beneath his black sweater. A strong face, sun-darkened and craggy, strong jaws. The way I wanted to look as a kid—except for the crazy, angry eyes.

I never wanted that hatred, that rage, that blackness in my gaze. I always wanted to be the hero, not the villain.

Just as he drags the screaming girl into his car, this scrawny little P.I. in his rain-soaked trenchcoat throws himself on the big guy's back. He is swatted away, his hornrim glasses flying, catching the light. The kidnaper roars away with the little girl in the car while the camera comes in on the P.I.'s face as he lies on the blacktop crying in the rain.

The P.I. wears my face. There on the TV. My face. He is me!

The image was already gone. A huckster was selling a car in living color, the sound blaring. I realized I was sweating. I lunged for my bottle. Empty. I sat there with it in my hands. I must have imagined the whole thing. Worn out from the emotional scene with Emily earlier, then the long drive, being unable to reach her, a couple of jolts of booze.

And I needed a couple more. I shrank the huckster to a white dot, to nothing. I didn't want to watch any more. Not hallucinating as I was. I still had on my coat and shoes, so I picked up the key off the dresser and went out into the rain.

I remembered passing a shopping mall, so I sloshed past the now-darkened motel office and down the narrow drive to the almost-empty acre of blacktopped parking lot. At the far end, warm yellow light shone out from a liquor store through almost horizontal windblown spears of rain. A pale Continental was just pulling up in front. A tall woman with pale hair to match the car, bare-headed in the rain, jumped out and ran inside, leaving her lights on and the motor running.

I slopped my way across the lot, shoulders hunched. It was a filthy night. I was soaked to the knees and water was running down my glasses, steaming them up. Wind whipped and tore at me. One especially heavy gust blew me sideways a couple of feet.

I reached the light-halo laid down through the store windows. Inside, the blonde was at the counter buying something that looked like cough medicine. That's when it happened.

A wide-stanced gleaming black sportscar spun around in a controlled skid, looking like the batmobile, its spinning wheels throwing out sheets of water. This huge dark shape hurtled from it and ran across the intervening blacktop to the blonde's Connie before the sportscar even stopped.

This time for real. This time in color and with sound. And with real sensations. I could feel the rain hitting my face. Could hear the slap of his soles against the blacktop, the sudden screams of the little girl as he reached across the front seat of the Continental and dragged her out with one thick arm.

Screams. Little arms stretching out to me for help.

I leaped.

Landed on the kidnaper's back like a monkey on a gorilla as he shoved the girl into the car, which was growling in rhythmic snorts like one of the big cats gearing itself for the charge.

A treetrunk arm sweeping me aside, in a myopic blur my glasses arching away from me, glinting in the falling rain, my room key flying from my hand, macadam slamming the side of my face, rain in my mouth, rolling over twice, a face looking down at me fleetingly.

That face. *The face from the television.* Bulging jaws, glittering eyes, heavy brows, a handsome, dissolute, vicious face, full of rage and fear and paranoia because he hated his father and feared women, feared their usurpation of his power, *how did I know that?* the mouth wide, perfect teeth gleaming.

Laughing. At me.

The car roaring away, huge and mythic from my ground-level viewpoint, acrid exhaust in my face.

Despairing cries from the open doorway of the liquor store, *"Em! Emmy!* Oh my God, *Emmy!"*

Salty tears against my lips. I had failed. But then up, on my feet, running as hard as I could through the rain after the car. Shouting something, only sounds, no words, no meaning.

Rage. For the first time in my life, blind rage. *"Come back and fight! You bastard! You bastard!"*

But the ersatz batmobile was gone. I stood there in the rain with water slamming my shoulders, running off my curled fingertips.

Defeated. Ineffective. Impotent.

The mother had called her *Em.* And then *Emmy.* Emily! I hadn't seen her face, but—No, I couldn't deal with that. This was *my* nightmare, not my Emily's little-girl nightmare.

And somehow it had been showing on my TV.

Real-life drama. On my television.

I snatched up my glasses and ran back toward my motel unit. I'd lost my key, but the door, swollen with moisture, hadn't closed all the way.

Snap! Slight crackle. The set warming up.

The picture springs to life. Black-and-white. No sound. Motel room. Arty shot, P.I. subjective camera suddenly swings to the door. Someone knocking?

I *hear* the knocking. How can I hear—

It was someone knocking at *my* door. In real life.

On the TV, the viewpoint camera hesitates, then moves to the door. A hesitant hand reaches into the frame to turn the knob.

I was at my own door, terrified at the same time that my hand of its own volition, already had opened the door.

On the TV, a man steps through the open door. Black rain slicker. Holding up a leather pocket case, flopped open to show a gleaming badge.

The man in my open doorway, streaming rain from his shiny black slicker and holding up his badge, said, "Lieutenant Kellerman. Police. We found your room key in the parking lot."

Two Lieutenant Kellermans. One in my room, one on the TV screen. The same man, both places. Only now the TV screen is blank. The set has gone dead.

The Plummer mansion was a huge old stone place with hardwood paneling, antique furniture, and oriental carpets that did little to soften the austerity. While Kellerman waited for the ransom call, I tried to get a composite of the kidnaper with the police IdentiKit. At the same time calling Emily, then Claire, and getting *her*. It was on speakerphone, so they could hear us, but by then I didn't care.

"Where are you?" Claire demanded. "Emily borrowed my car and is driving all over southern Minnesota trying to find you. I stayed here in case you called. She's in a frenzy. She's—"

"I'm in Plummerton at—"

"That's over a hundred miles away!"

"—the A-One Motel on the freeway access road. Tell her—" I'd been about to say, Tell her I'm finally getting a chance to be a hero, but, belatedly aware of the listening ears, I finished lamely, "Tell her I love her."

And hung up because Kellerman was making slashing gestures across his throat. He was a fleshy middle-aged man with bloodhound eyes and more hair in his ears than on his head. He was staring at me steadily. "Emily? Your wife's name is Emily?"

"Yes."

He was silent for a long time. Then in a flat voice he just said, "Quite a coincidence."

I turned the IdentiKit around toward him.

"I guess this is about as close as I can come."

He scanned it quickly, then turned and raised his voice to call through the open door into the next room.

"Mrs. Plummer? Could you come in here, please?"

The blonde woman came in. Despite being close to hysterics, she reminded me of Eileen Wade in *The Long Goodbye*, walking like a dream into the Ritz-Beverly Hotel bar, slim and tall in white linen and with hair that looked to Marlowe like the pale gold of a fairy princess. But her voice trilled with suppressed tension.

"Did he call? Do whatever he says! I'll pay anything! I just want—" she started to sob "—just want my baby back."

Kellerman said uncomfortably, "No call yet, Mrs.

Plummer. We'll do everything your way when it does come in." He gestured at the IdentiKit. "Meanwhile, Mr. Durant has given us an idea of what the kidnaper looks like."

She bent to study the composite, then shook her head regretfully. "N—no, I've never seen that man before."

"Damn," muttered Kellerman under his breath. He turned to me. "We all want to thank you, Mr. Durant," he said with a false heartiness, "for what you tried to do, and for this composite. Now I can have one of my men run you back to your motel."

The phone rang.

The plainclothes cop at the extension turned on the recorder and pointed at Mrs. Plummer.

"H—hello?"

With the speakerphone we could hear both sides of the conversation.

Harsh voice, like his laughter. "I know you got the cops there, but—"

"My baby, my Emily, is she—"

"Shut up! I only say it once. I want the jewelry you keep in the safe behind Old Man Plummer's portrait. All of it, including the star sapphire. I want the geek to deliver it."

"The geek? Who—"

"Little guy jumped on my back."

Kellerman was making gestures, mouthing silent words at her. She spoke hesitantly into the phone as she stared at him. "Why—him? What's—your connection with—"

"I know his face, know what he looks like. He's the only delivery boy I can be sure ain't a cop in drag. Send him back to his motel room to wait. I'll call again with the drop point."

They gave me the jewelry. I think Kellerman was suspicious I'd been in on it from the start, but what else could he do?

"Drive Mr. Durant back to the motel, Brian. Then wait outside in your car in case he needs some assistance. We wouldn't want him to lose all that jewelry, would we?"

As usual, I was of two minds: me and my shadow-figure, I guess Emily would have said, were in disagreement. My private eye wanted to be a bagman, but what Emily called the real me knew I'd blow this the way I'd blown the girl's rescue and that's why the kidnaper wanted me involved. *The geek.* At that moment, like Jacob Asch in Arthur Lyons' *Other People's Money*, I knew without a doubt that I was not Sam Spade.

The uniformed cop was talkative on the way back down the winding narrow blacktop driveway. He pointed out a tall stone tower, no longer used, completely separate from the huge rambling 37-room mansion. The original Plummer had housed a powerful telescope there for astronomical observations and had been a collector in the Hearst vein—except, said the cop, his manias had run to the dark side of man: weapons, armor, devices of torture set up in the dungeonlike basement of the tower.

"I guess he was the current Mr. Plummer's grandfather."

"There isn't any current Mr. Plummer," said the cop. "He was forty years older than—" a gesture with his thumb "—*she* is. His first wife committed suicide after their infant daughter was kidnaped and never returned."

"*Kidnaped?*" I exclaimed. "Then tonight was just a repeat of something that happened—"

"Twenty years ago. He wanted an heir in the worst way, so seven years ago he married *this* one. She got pregnant right after they were married." His expression was a leer. "And then was widowed when *this* kid was just a little baby." He added, "Because Old Man Plummer, *he* was murdered."

"Murdered?"

"In the tower basement. In a thing full of big spikes."

"An iron maiden?"

"Better—they could see the guy get it in this. Two big slabs full of spikes, opened like a book. From Spain in the Middle Ages, I guess. There's a mechanism that closes 'em like shutting that book. Balance wheels, somebody's gotta push a lever to get it going. Somebody did." Another significant pause. "*She* was in Chicago with the baby when it happened."

"Conveniently in Chicago?"

"You didn't hear me say it."

Back at my room I sat on the foot of the bed, still in my trenchcoat, drained. Maybe when the cops called with the drop location, I could still—Who was I kidding? If I couldn't stop the kidnaping when the TV had told me ahead of time what was happening, how could I stop it now?

Unless—

I began flipping through the channels. Nothing. Primetime dramas. Sitcoms. Cable movies. Phone-company commercial with a guy punching out a number on a phone, his back to the camera. The set looked like one of those European castles that have tours to pay their taxes.

But wait. The color fades. The sound goes dead. The guy turns toward the camera. Yes! Him!

My phone rang.

I hesitated, then snatched it up. *His* voice. Heavy and brutal, dripping testosterone. "It's time."

I prayed my voice wouldn't crack with my fear. "Oh, yeah?"

"Yeah. Just you and me. No cops. Or else."

On the TV screen, his long arm drags little Emily into the frame. He is grinning. He has one ham hand clamped around the back of her neck and he shakes her slightly. Her little head jerks back and forth dangerously.

On the phone her voice whispered, *"Please—"*

"Stop!" I yelled. "I'll come! I'll come! Where are you?"

On the TV they are in a sort of dungeonlike room, with stone steps in the background winding around a stone pillar from above. And in that instant I knew where they were.

But I said again, stalling for time, "Where are you?"

Because on the screen *I am creeping down those stairs behind him!* In my rain-darkened trenchcoat and fedora, a tire iron clutched in one hand, I am carefully, silently, trying to sneak up on him as he stands facing the camera.

"You know where I am," he said.

"Yes," I admitted. I am creeping across the tiles. Twenty feet behind him. Sixteen. "But how can I get out of the motel room? The cops are watching it."

Twelve feet. Ten. So slowly. So silently.

"Go out the bathroom window."

"My car's out in front. Next to the cop's car."

Eight. Six.

"Mine's in back," he said. "With the keys in it."

I raise the tire iron high overhead.

And he laughed into the phone as on the screen he whirls, grabbing my arm, twisting the tire iron away as if it's papier-mache. He hurls me across the room—which is full of the implements of war and torture.

Hurls me into a wedge-shaped contraption of great slabs with daggerlike spikes imbedded in it. They rip at my flesh through my trenchcoat as I am rammed between them.

To one side, massive gearwheels. And the lever! His

hands throw it. The camera follows him as he crosses to the slabs. They are slowly inching together. I am between them. As I watch, one of the spikes slowly, excruciatingly pierces my outflung hand and comes out the back of it. Blood. My mouth is open. I am screaming silently.

He is laughing. Silently.

But I can hear his laughter in the telephone.

"If you don't wanna come, it's the little girl who—"

"I'll be there!" I said.

He said: "You wouldn't quit. You wouldn't give up. So now one of us has to die. You know that, don't you, pal?"

I heard my own voice saying, "Yeah, I know that. Pal."

How did I know that?

A hundred yards below the barbered lawns draped over the top of the hill like green icing, a narrow, muddy, leaf-covered track went off around the back of the hill. I turned the low-slung black sportscar into it instinctively. It ended in a gravel parking area for the maintenance people. I got out. The tire iron was in the carpet-lined trunk.

What was I doing here? Was I crazy? I had just seen my own death on the television.

Since I knew where he was, I wouldn't come down the stone steps from above as he expected. Instead, I'd surprise him.

The rain whipped around me, splattered against the felt crown of my hat. I longed for a cigarette, although I'd never smoked one in my life. I realized I was terrified. *Terrified.*

My own death!

But then I remembered what Marlowe said in *The Big Sleep* as he drove away from the Sternwood mansion for the last time: "What did it matter once you were dead? You just slept the big sleep, not caring about the nastiness of how you died or where you fell."

I had to save little Emmy. Alone. Maybe even then I had some foreknowledge of who I had to save her from.

I left the ransom in the car—I knew he wasn't here for money. *How did I know that?* I moved across the sodden leaves to the sunken rear entrance to the tower. It had mossy, discolored stone flanking it and grass growing up between the underfoot flagstones. He wouldn't expect me to know about it.

How did I know that?

I'd known the old hand-hammered iron hinges would squeak slightly as I opened the heavy hand-carved oak door just wide enough to slip through sideways. There are advantages to being slight. Of course, if you were huge and muscular you didn't have to worry about making noise. You just did what you wanted.

Defied your father's authority.

Thwarted the terrible power and intelligence of Woman.

Well, what did you expect? Excluded, walled away. Nobody there with you but—*her.*

He'd always known about me. But until tonight I hadn't known about him. Now I did. That was my edge.

This doorway opened directly onto the basement floor. Dread implements of man's most awful pleasures were all around me. The only lighting was from smoky torches set in angled wrought-iron sconces fixed to the pillars that supported the tower. How had they furnished enough light for the video cameras that—

Wait! I hunkered down behind a pillar, my hand sweaty around the tire iron. *What I had seen on that TV screen hadn't happened yet!* It wasn't real yet!

Was I lying in the rain on the shopping-mall parking lot?

Or asleep in the motel-room bed, all this a dream?

Or with Emmy in our own bed, in the bonds of hallucination?

Or lying in a hospital bed, dying of a fatal concussion from the parking-lot confrontation?

I edged around the pillar to peer into the shadowed reaches of the basement. No sign of the girl or the kidnaper.

One of us has to die. You know that, don't you, pal?

Yes, I know that.

I edged past a rack with a great wooden wheel on which victims would be stretched and broken. A chair with short thick spikes on the seat and the back. An iron cage for dunking someone into boiling oil. Then, the modified iron maiden in which Plummer had died: two marble slabs partially open like a book, long cruel spikes gleaming.

Little Emmy ran toward me from the shadows, arms outstretched, crying out in fear. I dropped my tire iron clanking on the floor and crouched to scoop her into my arms. I was shoved violently from the side. I staggered to my feet, tried to turn again, was shoved again, *went between the slabs.*

Searing pain as the spikes dragged along my unprotected face and hands. Dozens of points ripping at my clothes.

I had seen my death on TV.

Little Emmy sat on the floor like a sack of potatoes. She was silent, drooping, no resistance in her, petrified by her terror. The hulking killer stood above me, laughing. "You thought you could beat *me?*"

"I *will* beat you," I said.

But he already had turned away to activate the mechanism. I was counting on that, shifting inside my ridiculously outsized trenchcoat. Painful points dragged across my flesh, but they were blunted by the heavy cloth. Shifting, working my arms out of the sleeves.

He pulled the lever. And laughed.

He didn't understand.

He had always known about me, but thanks to my Emmy I knew all about him, too. My beloved Emmy.

Rumbling, the great marble slabs began to shift, closing almost imperceptibly. I shrank, exhaled—if they entered me deeply enough to hold me, I was through. Already I could feel blood running. I was being skewered alive. But he had stepped closer, right in front of those gaping jaws of death.

He sneered, "You will die, and I—"

"Will die," I said. "I can live without you, but you—"

Enraged, he reached in to grab the front of my shirt. "What do you mean? I—"

I twisted out of the coat, dropped flat under the spikes, shoved his feet, *hard*. He tumbled forward between the slabs.

He cried out, spikes raking him. I was free! I turned back, cocked a leg, kicked with all my strength.

He screamed. The spiked jaws, closing inexorably, held him. Slowly, excruciatingly, one of the spikes pierced his outflung hand, came out the back of it. Blood. His mouth was open, he was screaming hoarsely.

I watched only a moment longer, then turned away and scooped up little Emmy in my arms. She would be all right. Bleeding from a dozen gashes, I went back out the sunken entrance and across the soggy lawn toward the distant lights and warmth of the mansion.

I think I fell a few times. I think I was crying.

But, finally, I was whole.

I opened my eyes in a sun-washed hospital room. My beloved Emmy stood beside the bed, watching me with loving eyes. She bent and kissed me. Her hair smelled of floral shampoo. She stepped back and looked at me and smiled.

Grinned, rather. And paraphrased Marlowe in *The High Window*—the only private-eye novel she'd ever read.

"In your part of town you're a pretty good man and if the business got made out of Tony instead, it would be strictly on the house. No profit."

I gave her back Pietro Palermo's lines, out of the side of my mouth as befit a man who ran a funeral home and several rackets. " 'Thatsa good. Tony. One funeral—on the house.' "

She kissed me again, longer, deeper this time. Then we talked. She had gotten there just after they found me on the rain-swept lawn with little kidnaped Emmy in my arms.

"You're a hero now, darling," she said. "Just as you always knew you would be. You were right and I was wrong."

"No—*you* were right. Terribly right. The kidnaper—"

"Escaped. But she got her daughter back, so—"

"The daughter was *you*, Emily. As a little girl. Somehow I broke through time to the *first* kidnaping twenty years ago. You were the Plummers' infant daughter and it was mixed up with—"

She shook her head. "Danny darling, you ought to rest."

So I told her all of it, from the beginning right down to the closing jaws of that deadly torture machine.

"But there was nobody in it!" she cried. "No body, no blood, nothing to indicate—"

"That's because he was—" I took a deep breath "—*me*."

"Danny—"

"My dark side. My shadow side. A massive projection just like you told me. So strong that after the fight I—I had to save you from *me*. I had to kill that part of me so it could reintegrate and—"

She burst out laughing. "Don't start with that psychobabble again. You're not one of my patients."

She didn't believe a word of it.

That's okay. We don't want any part of the Plummer millions. It's enough to know that I'm right. And whole.

I've started working out on the weight machines and I'm developing muscles. I'm doing a little sparring, too, and working with the heavy bag. I start karate-training next week. I don't wear my hornrims any more—no contacts, either. Don't seem to need either one of 'em.

As for our love life, well—who needs a blonde bombshell when you've got Emmy?

Meanwhile, the rescue of the little girl in Plummerton got a lot of ink, even in the Twin Cities papers. They never caught the kidnaper—you and I know why, pal, don't we?—but my phone has started ringing. This morning it was one of the big agencies in Minneapolis. They'd seen me on the *Today* show and wanted to know my rates.

"Five hundred a day plus expenses," I growled at the guy. My voice has deepened in recent weeks and I've had to start shaving twice a day.

"That's damned steep, Durant."

"So don't pay it, pal—you think I give a damn?"

The words hung on the wire between us. Then he said, in a sort of wondering voice, "My God, you're a hard man, Durant. You rescued that little girl, so I thought—"

"You thought wrong," I snarled. Then Phil Marlowe's words came to me. " 'If I wasn't hard, I wouldn't be alive. If I couldn't be gentle, I wouldn't deserve to be alive.' "

They're sending me the case. It's a big one.

A wandering daughter job.

My meat.

My beloved grandfather died while I was away at college, so I hitchhiked home from Notre Dame for his funeral, then wrote an angry little story I called "Epitaph." Years later I tried to redo "Epitaph" into a crime story with a lot of hidden emotion. Fred Dannay, half of the Dannay-Lee team that wrote as Ellery Queen, accepted the story for publication in Ellery Queen's Mystery Magazine—*then made me rewrite it three more times. In 1970 it won the MWA Edgar for Best Short Story of the Year.*

GOODBYE, POPS

I got off the Greyhound and stopped to draw icy Minnesota air into my lungs. A bus had brought me from Springfield, Illinois to Chicago the day before; a second bus had brought me here. I caught my passing reflection in the window of the old-fashioned depot—a tall hard man with a white and savage face, wearing an ill-fitting overcoat. I caught another reflection, too, one that froze my guts: a cop in uniform. Could they already know it was someone else in that burned-out car?

Then the cop turned away, chafing his arms with gloved hands through his blue stormcoat, and I started breathing again. I went quickly over to the cab line. Only two hackies were waiting there; the front one rolled down his window as I came up.

"You know the Miller place north of town?" I asked. He looked me over.

"I know it. Five bucks—now."

I paid him from the money I'd rolled a drunk for in Chicago, and eased back against the rear seat. As he nursed the

209

cab out ice-rimed Second Street, my fingers gradually relaxed from their rigid chopping position. I deserved to go back inside if I let a clown like this get to me.

"Old man Miller's pretty sick, I hear." He half turned to catch me with a corner of an eye. "You got business with him?"

"Yeah. My own."

That ended that conversation. It bothered me that Pops was sick enough for this clown to know about it; but maybe my brother Rod being vice-president at the bank would explain that. There was a lot of new construction and a freeway west of town with a tricky overpass to the old county road. A mile beyond a new subdivision were the 200 wooded hilly acres I knew so well.

After my break from the Federal pen at Terre Haute, Indiana two days before, I'd gotten outside their cordon through woods like these. I'd gone out in a prison truck, in a pail of swill meant for the prison farm pigs, had headed straight west, across the Illinois line. I'm good in open country, even when I'm in prison condition, so by dawn I was in a hayloft near Paris, Illinois some 20 miles from the pen. You can do what you have to do.

The cabby stopped at the foot of the private road, looking dubious. "Listen, buddy, I know that's been plowed, but it looks damned icy. If I try it and go into the ditch—"

"I'll walk from here."

I waited beside the road until he'd driven away, then let the north wind chase me up the hill and into the leafless hardwoods. The cedars that Pops and I had put in as a windbreak were taller and fuller; rabbit paths were pounded hard into the snow under the barbed-wire tangles of wild raspberry bushes. Under the oaks at the top of the hill was the old-fashioned, two-story house, but I detoured to the kennels first. The snow was deep and undisturbed inside them. No more foxhounds. No cracked corn in the bird feeder outside the kitchen window, either. I rang the front doorbell.

My sister-in-law Edwina, Rod's wife, answered it. She was three years younger than my 35, and she'd started wearing a girdle.

"Good Lord! Chris!" Her mouth tightened. "We didn't—"

"Ma wrote that the old man was sick." She'd written, all right. *Your father is very ill. Not that you have ever cared if any of us lives or dies. . . .* And then Edwina decided that my tone of voice had given her something to get righteous about.

"I'm amazed you'd have the nerve to come here, even if they did let you out on parole or something." So nobody had been around asking yet. "If you plan to drag the family name through the mud again—"

I pushed by her into the hallway. "What's wrong with the old man?" I called him Pops only inside myself, where no one could hear.

"He's dying, that's what's wrong with him."

She said it with a sort of baleful pleasure. It hit me, but I just grunted and went by into the living room. Then the old girl called down from the head of the stairs.

"Eddy? What—who is it?"

"Just a salesman, Ma. He can wait until Doctor's gone."

Doctor. As if some damned croaker was generic physician himself. When he came downstairs Edwina tried to hustle him out before I could see him, but I caught his arm as he poked into his overcoat sleeve.

"Like to see you a minute, Doc. About old man Miller."

He was nearly six feet, a couple of inches shorter than me, but outweighing me forty pounds. He pulled his arm free.

"Now, see here, fellow—"

I grabbed his lapels and shook him, just enough to pop a button off his coat and put his glasses awry on his nose. His face got red.

"Old family friend, Doc." I jerked a thumb at the stairs. "What's the story?"

It was dumb, dumb as hell, of course, asking him; at any second the cops would figure out that the farmer in the burned-out car wasn't me after all. I'd dumped enough gasoline before I struck the match so they couldn't lift prints off anything except the shoe I'd planted: but they'd make him through dental charts as soon as they found out he was missing. When they did they'd come here asking questions, and then the croaker would realize who I was. But I wanted to know whether Pops was as bad off as Edwina said he was, and I've never been a patient man.

The croaker straightened his suit coat, striving to regain lost dignity. "He—Judge Miller is very weak, too weak to move. He probably won't last out the week." His eyes searched my face for pain, but there's nothing like a Federal pen to give you control. Disappointed, he said, "His lungs. I got to it much too late, of course. He's resting easily."

I jerked the thumb again. "You know your way out."

Edwina was at the head of the stairs, her face righteous again. It seems to run in the family, even with those who married in. Only Pops and I were short of it.

"Your father is very ill. I forbid you—"

"Save it for Rod; it might work on him."

In the room I could see the old man's arm hanging limply over the edge of the bed, with smoke from the cigarette between his fingers running up to the ceiling in a thin unwavering blue line. The upper arm, which once had measured an honest 18 and had swung his small tight fist against the side of my head a score of times, could not even hold a cigarette up in the air. It gave me the same wrench as finding a good foxhound that's gotten mixed up with a bobcat.

The old girl came out of her chair by the foot of the bed, her face blanched. I put my arms around her. "Hi, Ma," I said. She was rigid inside my embrace, but I knew she wouldn't pull away. Not there in Pop's room.

He had turned his head at my voice. The light glinted from his silky white hair. His eyes, translucent with imminent death, were the pure, pale blue of birch shadows on fresh snow.

"Chris," he said in a weak voice. "Son of a biscuit, boy . . . I'm glad to see you."

"You ought to be, you lazy devil," I said heartily. I pulled off my suit jacket and hung it over the back of the chair, and tugged off my tie. "Getting so lazy that you let the foxhounds go!"

"That's enough, Chris." She tried to put steel into it.

"I'll just sit here a little, Ma," I said easily. Pops wouldn't have long, I knew, and any time I got with him would have to do me. She stood in the doorway, a dark indecisive shape; then she turned and went silently out, probably to phone Rod at the bank.

For the next couple of hours I did most of the talking; Pops just lay there with his eyes shut, like he was asleep. But then he started in, going way back, to the trapline he and I had run when I'd been a kid; to the big white-tail buck that followed him through the woods one rutting season until Pops whacked it on the nose with a tree branch. It was only after his law practice had ripened into a judgeship that we began to draw apart; I guess that in my twenties I was too wild, too much what he'd been himself 30 years before. Only I kept going in that direction.

About seven o'clock my brother Rod called from the doorway. I went out, shutting the door behind me. Rod was taller than me, broad and big-boned, with an athlete's frame—but with mush where his guts should have been. He had close-set pale eyes and not quite enough chin, and hadn't gone out for football in high school.

"My wife reported the vicious things you said to her." It was his best give-the-teller-hell voice. "We've talked this over with Mother and we want you out of here tonight. We want—"

"*You* want? Until he kicks off it's still the old man's house, isn't it?"

He swung at me then—being Rod, it was a right-hand lead—and I blocked it with an open palm. Then I backhanded him, hard, twice across the face each way, jerking his head from side to side with the slaps, and crowding him up against the wall. I could have fouled his groin to bend him over, then driven locked hands down on the back of his neck as I jerked a knee into his face; and I wanted to. The need to get away before they came after me was gnawing at my gut like a weasel in a trap gnawing off his own paw to get loose. But I merely stepped away from him.

"You—you murderous animal!" He had both hands up to his cheeks like a woman might have done. Then his eyes widened theatrically, as the realization struck him. I wondered why it had taken so long. "You've *broken out!*" he gasped. "*Escaped!* A fugitive from—from justice!"

"Yeah. And I'm staying that way. I know you, kid, all of you. The last thing any of you want is for the cops to take me here." I tried to put his tones into my voice. *"Oh!* The scandal!"

"But they'll be after you—"

"They think I'm dead," I said flatly. "I went off an icy

road in a stolen car in downstate Illinois, and it rolled and burned with me inside."

His voice was hushed, almost horror-stricken. "You mean—that there *is* a body in the car?"

Right.

I knew what he was thinking, but I didn't bother to tell him the truth—that the old farmer who was driving me to Springfield, because he thought my doubled-up fist in the overcoat pocket was a gun, hit a patch of ice and took the car right off the lonely country road. He was impaled on the steering post, so I took his shoes and put one of mine on his foot. The other I left, with my fingerprints on it, lying near enough so they'd find it but not so near that it'd burn along with the car. Rod wouldn't have believed the truth anyway. If they caught me, who would?

I said, "Bring up a bottle of bourbon and a carton of cigarettes. And make sure Eddy and Ma keep their mouths shut if anyone asks about me." I opened the door so Pops could hear. "Well, thanks, Rod. It *is* nice to be home again."

Solitary in the pen makes you able to stay awake easily or snatch sleep easily, whichever is necessary. I stayed awake for the last 37 hours that Pops had, leaving the chair by his bed only to go to the bathroom and to listen at the head of the stairs whenever I heard the phone or the doorbell ring. Each time I thought: *this is it.* But my luck held. If they'd just take long enough so I could stay until Pops went; the second that happened, I told myself, I'd be on my way.

Rod and Edwina and Ma were there at the end, with Doctor hovering in the background to make sure he got paid. Pops finally moved a pallid arm and Ma sat down quickly on the edge of the bed—a small, erect, rather indomitable woman with a face made for wearing a lorgnette.

She wasn't crying yet; instead, she looked purely luminous in a way.

"Hold my hand, Eileen." Pops paused for the terrible strength to speak again. "Hold my hand. Then I won't be frightened."

She took his hand and he almost smiled, and shut his eyes. We waited, listening to his breathing get slower and slower and then just stop, like a grandfather clock running down. Nobody moved, nobody spoke. I looked around at them, so soft, so unused to death, and I felt like a marten in a brooding house. Then Ma began to sob.

It was a blustery day with snow flurries. I parked the jeep in front of the funeral chapel and went up the slippery walk with wind plucking at my coat, telling myself for the hundredth time just how nuts I was to stay for the service. By now they *had* to know that the dead farmer wasn't me; by now some smart prison censor *had* to remember Ma's letter about Pops being sick. He was two days dead, and I should have been in Mexico by this time. But it didn't seem complete yet, somehow. Or maybe I was kidding myself, maybe it was just the old need to put down authority that always ruins guys like me.

From a distance it looked like Pops, but up close you could see the cosmetics and that his collar was three sizes too big. I felt his hand: it was a statue's hand, unfamiliar except for the thick, slightly down-curved fingernails.

Rod came up behind me and said, in a voice meant only for me, "After today I want you to leave us alone. I want you out of my house."

"Shame on you, brother," I grinned. "Before the will is even read, too."

We followed the hearse through snowy streets at the proper

funeral pace, lights burning. Pallbearers wheeled the heavy casket out smoothly on oiled tracks, then set it on belts over the open grave. Snow whipped and swirled from a gray sky, melting on the metal and forming rivulets down the sides.

I left when the preacher started his scam, impelled by the need to get moving, get away, yet impelled by another urgency, too. I wanted something out of the house before all the mourners arrived to eat and guzzle. The guns and ammo already had been banished to the garage, since Rod never had fired a round in his life; but it was easy to dig out the beautiful little .22 target pistol with the long barrel. Pops and I had spent hundreds of hours with that gun, so the grip was worn smooth and the blueing was gone from the metal that had been out in every sort of weather.

Putting the jeep in four-wheel I ran down through the trees to a cut between the hills, then went along on foot through the darkening hardwoods. I moved slowly, evoking memories of Korea to neutralize the icy bite of the snow through my worn shoes. There was a flash of brown as a cotton-tail streaked from under a deadfall toward a rotting woodpile I'd stacked years before. My slug took him in the spine, paralyzing the back legs. He jerked and thrashed until I broke his neck with the edge of my hand.

I left him there and moved out again, down into the small marshy triangle between the hills. It was darkening fast as I kicked at the frozen tussocks. Finally a ringneck in full plumage burst out, long tail fluttering and stubby pheasant wings beating to raise his heavy body. He was quartering up and just a bit to my right, and I had all the time in the world. I squeezed off in mid-swing, knowing it was perfect even before he took that heart-stopping pinwheel tumble.

I carried them back to the jeep; there was a tiny ruby of

blood on the pheasant's beak, and the rabbit was still hot under the front legs. I was using headlights when I parked on the curving cemetery drive. They hadn't put the casket down yet, so the snow had laid a soft blanket over it. I put the rabbit and pheasant on top and stood without moving for a minute or two. The wind must have been strong, because I found that tears were burning on my cheeks.

Goodbye, Pops. Goodbye to deer-shining out of season in the hardwood belt across the creek. Goodbye to jump-shooting mallards down in the river bottoms. Goodbye to woodsmoke and mellow bourbon by firelight and all the things that made a part of you mine. The part they could never get at.

I turned away, toward the jeep—and stopped dead. I hadn't even heard them come up. Four of them, waiting patiently as if to pay their respects to the dead. In one sense they were: to them that dead farmer in the burned-out car was Murder One. I tensed, my mind going to the .22 pistol that they didn't know about in my overcoat pocket. Yeah. Except that it had all the stopping power of a fox's bark. If only Pops had run to handguns of a little heavier caliber. But he hadn't.

Very slowly, as if my arms suddenly had grown very heavy, I raised my hands above my head.

~~DOLE~~
OLE
OLD
LED
DEL